THE OTHER SIDE

the other side

RENRUT .W. K

First printing edition 2022.

Published by Secret Freezer Publishing, PO Box 1025, El Mirage, AZ 85335
https://www.secretfreezerpublishing.com
https://kwturner.me

ISBN: 979-8-9870842-0-5 (Paperback)
ISBN: 979-8-9870842-9-8 (Paperback Alt)
ISBN: 979-8-9870842-4-3 (Hardcover)
ISBN: 979-8-9870842-6-7 (Hardcover Alt)
ISBN: 979-8-9870842-5-0 (eBook)

SECRET FREEZER

COMING SOON FROM K.W. TURNER:

2007

This is for The Penguin, The Lion, and the Shrimp.

Y'all my gatos and I will never, **EVER,** give up my goal to write your story.

TABLE OF CONTENTS

THE FOLLOWING EVENTS TAKE PLACE ROUGHLY BETWEEN **CHAPTERS P16 - P19** OF <u>TALES FROM THE JESSICA FILES</u>, BY PUNIS RUSSI.

THANK YOU FOR THE COLLABORATION, MY LIFELONG FRIEND.

I CAN ONLY HOPE FOR US TO DO THIS AGAIN, YOU SUPERVILLAIN!!!

SIGH, IF ONLY WE WERE RICH.

CHAPTER 0 – LOST

These writings are a story from a friend whom I hadn't spoken to in some time. I believe that they were lost in their mind, struggling. This is my translation of the story they presented to me and ghostwritten by myself with permission.

Most important to this story, there was genuine interest in hearing what my friend had to say, fascinated with the intricate nature of their thoughts and feelings, and unable to turn away as if watching a garbage truck on fire.

The question presented is this: How easy could it be to descend into hell if you don't have integrity or honor, lacking in compassion or morality, are completely lost in your mind—completely lost in life?

I often question whether I could slip up and fall down that slippery slope. What happens if I lose my integrity? What happens if I stop caring and allow apathy to take over? Who am I? What happens?

The starting point of this story is to notate and extrapolate, "Hey, this isn't an action movie script. This is not a fun-filled up and down action thriller".

No, this is all about my friend and how easy it would be for them to descend into a personalized hell. To be that which they do not want to be. To become something so awful that it gives them nightmares.

Personal note -> Throughout these writings, we will learn how that could happen to someone, how they could have lost it all, and how it could've quickly happened to them. And that's why I am writing this for my friend. He was forever lost in his mind trying to find the lost corundum he could not reassemble.

CHAPTER 1 – BACKSTORY

Chapter 1 of this story is probably backstory. I decided to share some thoughts I have generated and the craziness of my mind.

Recently I shared a blog post with a very close friend of mine, The Reverend C.D., and he was kind enough to give me a critique about it. The issue I was writing about was how much of a screw-up I feel like, and it was a rather lengthy post, about a thousand words.

I have been overly critical of myself over the last 1.5 to 2 years in my decisions and how I continue to live with the ramifications of such actions.

I'm delighted that I shared this with him; his feedback was fantastic, and below are two pieces of those thoughts. I won't break them down, I don't think, but I wanted to share.

"I know you're in a dark place most of the time. I understand the pressure. I wish I could do something to elevate your self-esteem and prop up your self-worth.

"The hardest thing for me to learn was self-forgiveness. It took a long time to cut myself a break on some dumbass choices I made. They still haunt me sometimes, especially when I'm feeling down. But I must remember that I am past that decision, and it's over— no going back. Still, I'm nowhere near perfect, so I, too, fall into that trap."

While I hadn't considered if the conversation would see the light of day, it is essential to note a few things that sometimes get overlooked, perhaps just unseen. These are parts of the story, in this case, the backstory.

The issues that I'm going through right now, along with millions of other people, I would add, are the feeling that the walls are closing in and that there are fewer and fewer options available.

What is all that mean? I'm sure that the average person can figure that out, and I'm not going into that part right now, but I want to highlight the feeling of helplessness that one can have when one has nothing. I want to quote Gerald Celente:

"When people have nothing left to lose, and they've lost everything, they lose it."

To me, that is like the walls starting to close in. And that quote is something that I have referred to or generally spoken about for many years. I believe that it has helped me keep some level of sanity in the insanity that is my life.

It was always an option in the recesses of my mind. The backstory continues.

I have nowhere to go if things were to get worse. I will eventually run out of money. I have nowhere to move. I have nowhere else to live. I have been concise and evident to those around me that I have no intent or willingness to be homeless.

I am not going to leave my gatos. That is a statement of fact, not an opinion.

One of the key aspects of this backstory is my gatos, my cats. The gatos are everything to me. Without them, I would have found the dark place a lot sooner. They give me hope as I make my way through the darkness.

But what happens when you start running out of options? What happens when you have nowhere to go or nobody to turn to because you are alone? That is my question, and that's why it is so important to set that in a backstory, to give context.

This issue has pushed my anxiety levels to new heights, and there is nothing that I can do for myself to help stem the rise or subdue it. Yet another point to the backstory.

What exactly does that mean? What exactly does that statement signify?

Years ago, I dated a gal in a very on-and-off relationship again. Very good human and somebody whom I am still friends with. I still play words with friends with her. A very worthy opponent who typically beats me, but that's another story.

Something that she beat into me that has severely affected my psyche was that, well, two things.

- One, you are not that special.
- Two, "Ain't nobody gives a shit about anything you have to say."

That is the main reason I have never really pushed myself very hard with my blog, and generally speaking, when I did write, I wrote to say whatever I wanted, not a story, let alone a backstory, because I don't care.

It was a humbling learning experience, much like many of the others I've had, where they were either incredibly painful or financially painful. Like getting married…

But it makes you realize that you're not special, just like everybody else and that nothing you do matters to anybody other than yourself. That has been a humbling experience because everybody wants to feel like they mean something to somebody.

Why am I going on and on about this? What is so important about that? Is it straightforward? It's not that simple. That's why it's' called a backstory. Yes, a backstory.

She explained to me while we were together, as well as after our relationship ended, that the intent of the comment wasn't to be hurtful or mean but to help me come down from my high horse where I thought that I was much better than everybody else, (which I was IMO), and that reality dictates differently.

That was a very eye-opening experience to be told that… to have that said to you. Some 6+ years later, the damage to my brain has multiplied and, in some regards, been incredibly crippling—a replicating, viral disease intent on destroying me.

I've long thought about this conversation, how it made me feel, and cost me an opportunity with someone, and that bothered me. It was further fuel to the fire of self-doubt and despair.

The statement made by that ex has stayed with me and still haunts me now. It has negatively impacted several functions of my life. And the two most notable would be jobs and relationships.

And that is the end of the **backstory**. There will be more to come...

CHAPTER 2 – HOPE WITH A SIDE OF FEAR

There is always hope when you have fear; there always needs to be hope. There is nothingness in life. It's like a Nine Inch Nails song stuck in my head.

As we stood in the kitchen, my buddy Fry made some drinks as I prepared to start making dinner. This was the first time that we'd gotten together in some time. I promised Fry to tell him this story for a while now, and I was eager to start.

"I do not want to be that person who ends everything," I said as I started to wash up the salad fixings. "I don't want to live with the specter hanging over my head.

"This is a very long dissertation on being a good person and how easy it is to fall prey to evil. The very thought, the very notion that one can turn evil in such an easy manner, is unfathomable. I would further suggest that it is super saddening." That was hard to get out.

I continued, "That's the overall theme as if it wasn't obvious. I've said over fifty times over the years. At the end of my nightmares, there is blackness. There is no light, and there's no hope, nothing."

I thought I could not allow that to happen for myself or the gatos. That echoed in my mind for a while as I put the now-cleaned veggies into the colander, allowing them to dry off a little.

Fry motioned me to my drink, a concoction so simple and delicious that I couldn't resist the temptation to gulp down half the glass of Cromulent Vodka/Zevia (with some lime to prevent scurvy).

"I can't let that happen for myself," I continued. "The people of this country and all of the world's citizens. This is not a threat, and it's not a manifesto, not an instruction guide. It's just a way to talk about a personal hell. I hope that I'm not going there in the first place.

"Hope is a multi-faceted gem, as seen with the hope diamond. Hope comes in many forms and is implemented in many different methodologies." I was starting to wonder if I could get this all out tonight.

"Hope can also come from finding something you have lost, like a multi-faceted gem you misplaced."

Fry interrupted me, noting, "Dude, we both know what was lost can never be returned. You know the context as well as I do. I wish you'd..." before trailing off.

I took another sip of my drink and searched for some coconut oil to season my bamboo cutting boards, biting my tongue about Fry calling me dude. He knew I hated that.

"To continue my original thought... Hope can come from religion. Hope can come from family. Hope can come from a spiritual leader or your faith. Hope can come from somebody you emulate or adore, a celebrity or a role model.

"Just a note; because I want to be a dick, I don't believe that there are very many celebrities or (air quotes) "famous people" (air quotes) that should be emulated or looked to as a standard-bearer of any sort of hope.

"When you have people who are only interested in money, power, and wealth," I continued. "When you have people like that, there is no hope. Our society is falling apart because there is no hope.

"For fuck's sake, we have rappers who shoot people, often killing them, and we hold them at a higher reverence than people who cure a major disease."

I paused for a second and looked over to Fry; he didn't look as if he was glossed over yet, so I continued.

"Having no hope is the beginning of a recipe for disaster" I proclaimed as I was working on the cutting boards. "Without hope, you could easily slide into fear, suffering, and despair that leads to pure evil. Ok, I feel better now that I've gotten that little rant out of the way," I noted. My brain says to get back on track.

"A few days ago, I was awoken by the gentle meows of Bugsy. That was because he wanted to be fed, even though it was 3:30 in the morning. I sighed through my nose to profess my displeasure with his request. He didn't care.

"Annoyed, I got out of bed and took a quick bio break.

"When I turned around, Bugsy had enlisted his cohorts, Koni and Yags. The three were sitting there at attention, looking at me like I was fucking with them.

"I took a deep breath and quietly mumbled something about Ambien and dying while walking down the stairs.

"So, we made our way to the stairs. I paused on the third step, hoping that the clowns would start down and therefore be less likely to make my dope ass crash and burn down the stairs.

"It seemed all safe to proceed, and I got halfway down when Bugsy stopped and flopped down onto the stair in front of me. What a dick!

"I step around him, giving him the ole half-opened eyes and a smirk that says, 'Sucka, can't get me.' Today will be fun, you fucks!

"I fed Bugsy, Koni, and Yags and went back to bed, hoping to get more than 3 hours of sleep before I was awoken again."

I walked to the cutlery drawer and slowly took out a standard eight-inch knife. "Shit, I need to get these knives sharpened. Not like I haven't been saying that for years."

We both chuckled as Fry made the turn to make another drink. "You ready for another?" he asked me.

"Fuck yeah!" and I slammed the rest down. "I love only having one giant two-inch ice cube! It's always good for two drinks."

As Fry made the drinks, I took a minute to use the frequently loud sharpening stone to ensure good cuts tonight.

"I hate that disappointing feeling you get when faced with a lack of continuous sleep. This whole multiple-times-a-night escapade Bugsy is getting on my fucking nerves. And because of that, it's making me grumpier each day."

By the time I had finished sharpening the knife, Fry had motioned to come to get my drink. We tend to fill them right up to the brim, where you can't pick them up. So, it's a slurp or two, and then you are on your way.

Fry took his drink, went to the kitchen table, and sat down. I could tell he wasn't bored but very thankful that there was alcohol. That's not uncommon.

I grabbed some of the veggies and started to chop away in hopes of not cutting off a finger while talking away. Typically, it's the other way around, where Fry tells me a fantastic story, and I listen to it while cooking.

"I have faith in myself" I proclaimed as I was getting back into the story. I smiled as I thought, damn, that was a hard turn.

"This will sound outrageous, but I'd like to end the story here in a minute, not because I don't want to talk about it, nor that I am worried about losing a finger in the process, but..." And with that, I started to trail off with my thoughts.

"This'll be a great time for me to step outside and have a hit on the vaporizer. Does that sound good?" Fry asked.

"Sure, I'll keep working on the salad." Fuck, that sounded stupid.

Fry is a great friend; I know he doesn't always enjoy how dark I can be when speaking. And that's regarding the fact that I'm incredibly open and honest and am always willing to discuss something. And Fry knows the complete backstory of what we're talking about

But still, he does not want to hear it when I talk about some of these topics. I respect that, and I felt like I would start down that road, knowing that this would be a long conversation. Not in terms of today but... but it's something that I will have to reveal to him over the next few weekends when we have dinner.

Fry has had to deal with my relationship problems with the various exes, and he's had to listen to some rather gory details therein. That's why he's my best friend.

And that leads into the last part I was going to bring up when Fry comes in from his smoke break. I wouldn't say I like the sound of that fucking device. I've forced him to go outside now. It also allows him time to fiddle with his phone, likely texting with his girlfriend.

I continued with the salad, my mind focused on the task at hand. I got everything set for final eating preparations when Fry came back in.

Fry sat down at the table as I worked on getting it set with the appropriate utensils for the evening.

"Please continue your last statement about faith," Fry noted.

"I have faith in myself," I repeated.

"I have faith in myself, and I have faith in my convictions. I believe that my strength is beyond comprehension and that my will is more potent than imagination. I can handle anything that is thrown at me. I've stared down anger and hatred, knowing all the time that I was better than that.

"I knew I was a human, not built on hatred or living with hate. I never want to be that person.

"I think it's essential that when you have faith, it is first and foremost in yourself. If you have faith in a creator, that's great. If you have confidence in some object or a tangible asset, that's great too.

"My feelings on the topic of faith stem from a straightforward principle of libertarianism, which is not an official party policy." And with that, I rolled my eyes, annoyed by having said that.

"Generally speaking, I don't give a fuck what people do, so long as it doesn't impact me, it doesn't hurt children, it doesn't harm the elderly, nor does it harm animals. Otherwise, if it's within the scope of the law, I don't care... do your thing."

I put the salad fixings together, handed Fry off the plate, gave him the pepper mill, and sat down to eat.

I paused to ensure that this philosophy about humanity was adequately registered. "I don't think this week is the right time to continue, so I'm going to leave it there with my generalized philosophy," I said and then stuffed my mouth full of salad.

As we ate, all I could hear aside from the sound of us destroying some vegetables was Every Day Is Exactly The Same; it haunted me.

CHAPTER 3 – FEAR WITHOUT HOPE

Fear without Hope... Fry was over again for our weekly dinner and conversations. I dominated the discussion last week and felt guilty, but this is all about me.

I was looking forward to continuing the story and getting Fry further up to speed. The following events were on the second Saturday. And on we go.

While waiting for Fry to get here, I was thinking about some pressing topics in my mind. "How do you excel? How do you become more exceptional than everybody else to stand out so that you have more, perhaps better, access to resources?"

I know the answers, I think. Maybe I suppose I know them. I continued to ponder as I waited for the moderate boom of the bass from Fry's vehicle. It was never obnoxious, something the neighbors at the various houses I have rented have suggested or complained about in those neighborhoods.

I don't want to be a dick, but we don't always have the same taste in music. But that's OK. I tell myself repeatedly that I accept him for more than his musical tastes, a sure sign of growth as a human. Sadly, I'd very much question the validity of that statement.

I continued my inner monologue. By resources, I mean better jobs, better career paths, better partners when it comes to relationships. I have always managed, at least in a business sense, to have gainful employment, even though I have been subject to downsizing several times.

Fry knew all of this; we'd discussed them in many places and ways. This is why I'm talking to myself about it. I always fear that bringing it up will be a problem.

Sometimes that is just a numbers game like with companies like PROC LIVE. Those losers, I added to my thoughts. I smiled to myself as Fry pulled into the driveway.

Sometimes it's a different type of numbers game, like when another employer lays off two-thirds of their staff because there were inappropriately handling their funds.

Oh, that action covers many places.

I don't mean this to be rambling; I'm just trying to give context to where and why things are.

All this rambling and information has to do with feeling like the walls are closing in, spurring all sorts of panic attack-like emotions. And much like millions of other people, as I said earlier, I'm in a position where I have been unemployed for 7+ months.

I have a finite amount of money and previously lived a pretty good lifestyle. I seemingly have no way to resolve the perception of parts of my soul being ripped away from me slowly, methodically, and with malice.

When I was laid off, it took between seven and eight weeks to get unemployment, and during that time, the unemployment pay in Arizona was capped at $240 a week.

If you know anybody who can survive on $240 a week who is an adult and lives in a house or an apartment, I would love to talk with them, and I would like to hear their story.

At that point, the Federal government was kicking in $600 a week for unemployment across the board, and once I got my unemployment check, I had a full two weeks of that.

Then that disappeared, and El Presidanté signed an executive order allowing for an additional $400 a week. Whereas the State of Arizona took/didn't give $100 of that, providing unemployed workers an extra $300/week.

I was optimistic that I could survive and make it work. It was in the hope that I could get another similar job in the tech world, in terms of pay and functionality, utilizing my skills more so than the last clown shop.

And in this time, my hope of finding a job has continued a slow but sure decline to the point where it is seemingly never going to happen.

You apply for 25 jobs in which you are qualified and hear back from none.

You continuously get job information emails from "recruiters" that are entirely outside your skillset and are so unrealistic that you have to question the mental acuity of the clown shoes sending you this email because they either cannot read or have no comprehension skills, but that is another topic.

I tend to lean on the stupidity factor, but what do I know?

From a market perspective, I have seen that the frequently listed jobs that fall within the scope of my skill set seemed to have dropped pay by at least $25,000 yearly, if not more.

And that's yet another hard pill for myself and millions of others to swallow. But it harkens me back to where I grew up and when PROC LIVE, those fucktards, those assholes, laid off a substantial number of employees in the area where I grew up.

And what happened was the market collapsed. You had people with masters of electrical engineering who were proverbially fighting for a job at Home Depot and making minimum wage.

And that was disheartening, partly because I was 18 then. I felt like I could see the future, fearfully knowing what could come to pass.

I don't mean that to sound like a prophet; I could see the writing on the wall that where I grew up would not be a sustainable location to live and have a career. And even though I wasn't entirely sure what that career path would be, I knew it would not be there.

And slowly but surely, I could pull myself out of that shit with some help from family, and I moved out here to Arizona when I was 22. I had no job or car but a place to live.

I didn't panic because I was 22 and knew I would have opportunities ahead of me. I was afraid of failure, but I knew it was inevitable; I was young enough that I could learn from it, rebound, and become stronger.

Today, not 22, I know that those opportunities are behind me. I understand that this isn't just my feelings but something relatively common that happens to people in my age bracket.

Why hire somebody at $50,000 a year when you can pay somebody $25,000 a year and train them? Ahh, Globalism.

The only folks not fucked over by that philosophy are the ones enriching themselves with such greed that it astounds one to think of how many lives they are destroying to have more of that sweet, sweet green.

While one could presume that that is age discrimination, it's just a business fact, and I fear it is challenging to prove. I digress.

Moreover, this whole thing drives down values and all the other things that come with it. Think of it as the housing market.

On top of that, the collapse of the employment market falls into capitalism. It plays off of my last comment. When you have a surplus of something and the demand increases, you can set the rates better. Think of real estate; that's my best example because the prices decrease when you have more houses than people; when you have more people, house prices go up.

General market dynamics, and that is what is going on right now. I see in the job market that you are applying for a job, and a hundred people already have.

These recruiters must be completely overwhelmed, and it's hard to do your due diligence in looking at every potential applicant when you have 100 people posting for one position in the first few hours. It reminds me of my grandparents' stories about the Great Depression.

This is a significant market issue, and even if the economy is starting to come back, it's going to take time for people with a higher employment rate, salary-wise, to find positions that are remotely close to it, and this is what happened where I grew up. Still, it never truly recovered, and if you wanted to make money there in Minnesota, you had to travel to Minneapolis to make that type of money.

Generally, that meant at least three hours a day of commute time. Just think of that: every day, at least three hours of your day are pissed away sitting on a train or bus or something.

But that was what people had to do there, at that time, and I'm sure, like now, a lot of those people felt very panicked due to "What am I going to do to feed my kids and put a roof over their head?"

Again, I know this is rambling, but there is a point to all of this. The general point I'm trying to get across to everybody is a twofold issue here; nay, let's say they are multifaceted cluster fuck, a gem of another name.

I don't know how I'm going to be able to manage this because, as I said, there's a limited number of jobs, unemployment funds, and money. That's my inner fear seeping out. Fear that I will lose hope.

I don't own a house, I rent, and I have continued to pay my rent per my lease agreement, but I have another year.

That creates problems because even if I wanted to move somewhere with lower rent, I can't do that with no job. Even if my current landlord is pretty awesome, it is improbable to happen.

Nobody will rent a house or apartment to somebody with no job. I hate to say that, but you'd be pretty naïve if you did. No offense.

I also have a problem: Phoenix is a vast metropolitan area where everything is built outwards rather than upwards. That means I could not reasonably get rid of my car, which is also rather costly/expensive.

I have worked with my auto loan lender and have gotten a couple of months pushed back, but I'm at the edge of where I can continue to do that. And with a finite amount of resources, you start having to look at how you will survive.

Yes, I realize I have gone in a circle, which is part of my intent. I hope I can get out of this, but I also have to be prepared that I might not be able to.

I know that that is very dark. And I don't mean it to be, per se, but the reality is what reality is, and I'll quote a Dream Theater song: The truth is the truth, you just gotta live with it.

So, where does this go from here? I ask again, where does this go from here? And that is the critical question. You can continue to bang your head against the wall, or you can just not try.

I don't know which is where I am, but I know that no matter what, the walls will have to crush me to make me give up.

But I did know one thing… I sure as fuck get out of a car faster than this shit show. But he's my best friend.

And it was just then that I realized I was standing there like a dork, having conversations with myself in my head and not helping him. Sigh. I'm the ass douche now.

As I went over to help Fry, trying to smile my way around my transgression of standing there lost in my brain, I realized that there was so much to talk about still, and I wasn't going to be afraid of it.

That's my greatest fear in this, I think. The fear of being fearful about the sheer amount of fear that I am staring down. And that's how to do it.

———————————————————————————

CHAPTER 4 – FEAR WITH DARKNESS

Fear. Darkness. I know what's coming, and I have tried to prepare my friends and family for it, but I have been preparing for the inevitability for several years.

It's the saddest situation and a sad statement. This, too, is the darkness.

Fry and I were sitting in the kitchen once more. He was sitting at the kitchen table and taking puffs off his god-awful e-whatever fucking thing.

I was washing up some petite potatoes at the sink that would be a part of dinner.

In the back of my head, I heard myself saying, "Dude, what's the fucking recipe for this shit? ... Oh, so neither of us knows? FUCK!" Yeah, mental health issues are a bitch.

We had the Cromulent Vodka/Zevia flowing. I took a swig, perhaps you could call it a gulp, and I politely asked, "Is now a good time to continue with 'The Story'?"

With a nod, it was time. I've always loved how a nod and glance portray the appropriate answer.

I'd been thinking about this a lot, and I knew I was getting to some parts where the darkness started coming out. I don't want to allow my darkness to consume me.

These chats with Fry have helped ease some of this fear and pain.

"I've continued thinking about what it takes to admit to yourself that you were not only a failure but a monumental failure and that I have failed everybody and everything." I know that was a bold statement to start based on the look I got.

I paused for another swig of my drink before looking around for the fixings I needed for these petite potatoes. I think that's what they are called.

Super tasty and easy to cook in the oven and seasoned the way we'd grown accustomed. Not that I have a cookbook deal, but Special Shit is the shit.

"Let's talk about failure. You damn well know my mother had told us, my two sisters and I, and yourself and Ms. J, that she had intended to kill herself and detailed precisely how.

A few years ago, as you recall, when she passed away, my sisters and I completely believed that that was what she had done. No doubt."

Whew. That was another big statement; I thought to myself as I spun around in the kitchen, looking for a Ziploc bag, the Special Shit Spices, and the olive oil.

I added, "This is to reiterate there was not a gambling-related thing; no, it was to when she'd die, how she'd die, and the generalized context of her death." I could feel the darkness starting to paw at me.

I started chuckling after that... It took me a good 10 seconds to stop. "I know; I had the under on all three! I talk such shit and mean it, especially about her. You know this to be true," I added.

I took another "sip" of my drink and took a deep breath, trying not to chuckle further.

"So... Good sister and I had been texting back and forth, and I mentioned to her that I was planning on using a small amount of the money on LegalZoom."

I know Fry is fully aware of what that means, so I had no reason to express anything on that topic for some stupid ass reason. Call it fear of the darkness I try to control. Or call it two dudes talking and having a few drinks.

"I'm not plugging them. I just want to ensure that I have a properly documented power of attorney, will, trust, all of that legal stuff because...".

So, there it was. The darkness is starting to creep up. Fear in my heart manifests itself as darkness. And no one likes the darkness inside another, nor wants to hear about it. Darkness is hard shit.

"I'm only telling you this because we need to understand where my mind is when making a decision that would inevitably lead me to where nothing good happens.

"Are you good for me to continue?" I asked. The response, another nod, and a hit off that fucking e-cig, whatever the fuck it is. "I'll continue, but this might be a little longer...."

"Last week, while talking with my doctor, we discussed some of the feelings I have been expressing lately. I'm not in a bad way where she scolded me, but she said something to me that was so striking about my willingness to go through with it."

Fry knew what that meant, his facial expressions changing based on the topic.

"It wasn't a challenge, and she made that very clear, and I agreed that it was not a challenge. But in all honesty, the honest answer is yes. I am prepared to because that's where my choice ends up."

"Just the other day, I was engaged in a conversation with my ex-wife, and we were talking about my current situation, and she was offering up some ideas and whatnot. I just reiterated to her that, the same thing that I had said to my therapist, that I have been preparing to because...."

And I trailed off in my mind. Yes, a lot of this topic... this topic, in particular, comes from my apathy and just how tremendously it had grown over the last few years, starting with leaving one company and where I had four jobs in twenty years. Since then, I have had three jobs in three years.

The dynamics of the technology field I specialize in have changed considerably. Where I was a systems engineer at the lead or senior level, that has changed from actual engineering like infrastructure design and implementation to more of a DevOps role. I have a hard time with DevOps because I feel my mental capacity to deal with DevOps is low.

The DevOps world is more about automation and scripting and continuous integration of pipelining and shit like that. That's not what I enjoy doing, nor is it within the passages of my mental capacity. I just don't understand it enough.

I don't know how long I paused with that in my mind, but I think it's time to start the grill so I can shut the fuck up for a few. Fry did not like where this was going.

"So, what I was saying to my ex-wife was how my experiences over the last few years and the inability to find a job going on 4+ months now, in many ways, is because I don't have some of the skills that these companies are looking for."

Fry finally added to the conversation with a very explicit statement. "You are so skilled that it's retarded that you are thinking some of this shit! You are a leader, not a follower. We've known this for a long time now."

"You aren't wrong," I added, and after a short pause, I continued, "This is where my fear takes me. The darkness is brought upon by the fear of having to make shitty job choices in going for the money and not the joy.

"I'd like to get back to my ex-wife if that's OK...." I nodded to Fry, and he got the door for me as we started firing up the grill outside. He had been seasoning both ribeye steaks for the last bit, and I wasn't paying attention as I was blathering about.

"I have tried to help my ex-wife understand the level of apathy that I am suffering from and what that means because she has always been the type of person who thinks that health changes people by giving them self-esteem.

"I knew and understood that she was giving me her honest position, and I have never guessed that was anything aside from positive intent. I know that she's not doing it to be an asshole." Under my breath, I chuckled, "That was my job.

"She asked me if I knew when the apathy took over, and in an instant, I told her when it consumed me; I think you may recall it. Day after Christmas, a few years ago. The girl from the grocery store...."

That raised an eyebrow or two from Fry as he fired up the grill. He's a fucking steak-grilling master, always perfect to what I want. A magical meat magician. OMG, that's so fucking funny!

"One night, I will talk about the girl from the grocery store; I think it will make for a good story.

"By the end of the conversation, I think my ex-wife was starting to understand that I have lost so much, as have so many other people. I've had to go through this process of not feeling sorry for myself and dealing with selling and getting rid of things I don't want to, but that's part of being an adult, apparently."

This is one of the parts that hurt me the most: things I had worked so hard to get. Some took over ten years to be able to obtain them finally.

"As you know, I just sold my best computer monitor, my best in-the-ear earbuds. I sold my Apple Watch and have one of my speaker amps for sale. I have a Schitt digital-to-analog converter (DAC) that is phenomenal and up for sale too. And that's just the beginning because I will have to make more sacrifices."

Fry got a call from work, and I stepped inside and shut the door, trying to give him privacy. I mean, I think it was from work. I mean, doesn't everyone call their co-workers sweetie and honey?

My mind went sideways with the chance to dance around the edges of the darkness. It's a joyful task if I do say so myself.

Fry came back in; I looked over to him, gave him a questioning nod, and got an approving nod.

"A few days ago, I was getting my haircut from my stylist of the last 20+ years. She and I were talking about the same general topic as earlier. She told me I was acting selfishly and that I should be looking at any possible jobs, even if it's a help desk position, just so I have extra money coming in.

"I sadly told her the same thing I had told my ex-wife. I just don't care. I'm at the point where I have been beaten down by so many people that I just don't care. How do you survive when you don't care about anything?"

And there it was, my brain popped. Darkness. Boom. "All of this is a part of the general downward spiral I am currently experiencing. It's an important part of the overall story because it is a complicated topic for people to discuss. Many times, people don't know what to say.

"In a funny bit, I was on Tinder recently, and as I looked through profiles (predominantly swiping left), I landed on a gal whose profile blurb was rather interesting.

"It felt like I knew this woman, but I have no idea why. She had a shirt in one of her pictures that said 'Suicide.' I thought it was funny because of where I am and how hard I try to keep the darkness in check."

I continued, "I'm pretty sure her name was Ms. E, and I knew her from a previous employment gig. At one point, I knew she was doing a pet sitting service, and I always considered that if I had traveled but… to no difference."

We both knew I fucking hated traveling. My knees never appreciated sitting in the economy section, so I flew first class. Fuck that. Too painful and too expensive.

"All of this, as I have learned, is the readiness I have as part of the story about what's going on in my life. Ultimately, it's selfish, but all I want to do is to protect myself and the gatos from the extraneous circumstance of what could be.

"One of the things that I have been thinking about, besides taking a shitty, shitty, shitty help desk level job, was something that my hairstylist mentioned to me.

"Maybe I could also look at a driving service like Amazon Delivery or BevMo, as examples, where I don't have to be around people, which is a fabulous thing for me because I don't like people."

Fry knew how much I disliked people. Darkness sets in when I think about taking them all with me. And some glee always came from the idea of doing that. Not that I have the means. Or energy, fuck that.

"I feel a rant coming on... I just spent $675 on maintenance for the fucking BMW because I was three months behind on a slew of services... oil change, air filter, brake fluid, coolant, and who the fuck knows what else was done.

"I don't want to talk to good sister about the money as this was one of those things that I told her I had to do. Do I use this as an opportunity to skip out my $214 a week from the state of Arizona because there's no fucking hope that the politicians in Washington, all those cunts, are going to get anything done that we would provide me with some relief? And I just don't care.

"I completely do not care. I don't care if I work. I've been enjoying writing the book. I have enjoyed working on blogging while paying more attention to leveraging SEO plugins formula to learn more."

"It has been great and interesting to me, but... That's not going to pay the bills, and if I want to stay in this house, I will have to figure out a better solution because I can't pay the retarded amount of money."

Fry knew that I was hitting hard in the fear area. I could sense he was seeing it in me.

"I have gotten apathetic to the point where I don't care about much of anything, including myself. I very obviously care about and love the gatos. I don't care what people say, I don't care what people think of me, I don't care about any of it, and it's just my apathy running rampant."

There, I said it. I brought the darkness to the fear and the fear to the darkness—a perfect circle of a downward spiral.

"It made me very nervous because there is always a possibility I can make my way through where I am right now and find a way to make it work. But I don't know what that looks like, and I wonder if I can do it every day."

"And with that, I know I have gone over the limits of what I could talk about with you tonight and am very appreciative…."

And I trailed off for a couple of seconds as I mentally added, "That you didn't put my head in the grill and slam the lid down a few times."

"I probably knew that about 15 minutes ago and didn't shut the fuck up. My apologies," I added, feeling shitty for having gone on and on.

I concluded the evening with, "Hey, how about some refills and you school me again on the proper steak-grilling process?"

CHAPTER 5 – DARKNESS AND HOPE

Lately, I have been feeling rather hopeless about how the tone can change around here. And it becomes worrisome. Worrisome because of the darkness. It feeds into my fears.

The idea of having a roommate makes me nauseated. I hope that's the right word for it. The last time I lived with somebody was back in 2008. I had a male roommate who was a referral that my ex-wife gave me.

My ex-wife knew that I needed a roommate. She would suggest that it was more needed than wanted, but she was always trying to be a good human. She had positive intent.

She had met him at an indoor soccer game, a league she and I played in. She was always chatting with everybody because that was her way.

Let's say his name was Cass. Cass was Canadian, just a very relaxed, smart guy and a good human. So, I want that to be the focus here, and I hope that comes across.

It wasn't so bad, but man, I fucking hated having somebody else around. It wasn't about Cass, and it was that darkness I have that consumes me and pushes me to hide. I didn't want to be hiding from Cass, but that would often happen.

Like my ex-wife, I know Cass didn't love that I'd get home and go into my office. I'd decompress for an hour or so, depending on how craptacular my day was. That was less about my ex-wife or Cass.

While having a roommate wasn't horrible because of Cass's personality, the extra money was excellent. But I had a $2000 mortgage payment, and he gave me $500 monthly. So while it helped some, it didn't help that much.

If I said, "But that's 25%, dude," I would be forced to slap myself.

And cue the shitty inner monologue.

All of this is ultimately my fault because I took some job or made life decisions that were inconsistent with what I should be doing, and therefore I have to pay the price for them. I hope that makes sense.

I thought it would have a different direction in my life, just like everyone else. I thought I was getting away from the darkness, but I wasn't. Instead, the darkness pulled me back in, no matter how far I ran.

Now I have this big fucking house that I'm renting. I bought a new car, which required me to trade my diesel BMW 335d, which I had paid off. Thus, it got me nowhere. I've gone nowhere. Sigh.

In a moment of sadness and self-realization, I have now decided to start applying for jobs where I am so incredibly overqualified that the likelihood of getting an interview is minimal. On top of that, any offer would be so minimal.

That is because no sane manager or director will hire somebody with 15 years of experience, highly specialized, for a job where they're answering emails all day for customer support. It's just stupid.

My alternatives, though, are nearly as unappealing. I have to figure out how to bring home a certain amount of money, just like everybody else. I have to figure out a way to survive because my ultimate goal here is not to kill myself.

The ultimate goal is to get back to where I was, but if I get to that point and I know, I know what I have to do.

I hope that later on in this book, I comment on or notate on my fears of suicide because I enjoyed Dante's Inferno immensely. And in the darkness, that would take me to the seventh level. That isn't a hotel and was not a destination where hope or delusion would save them from the darkness that they could not escape.

I thought about it one day and mentioned the topic to The Reverend C.D. He's one of the few people I look up to, and I have the utmost respect for him. He's a super fantastic human, and I value his opinion immensely.

He asked me, "Why is it you believe in the writings of one historian spinning a tale and yet not another?" Now that's a thought-provoking and introspective question if I've heard one.

I recall this happening when we were at the cemetery, so his comment had more weight on it than usual. It's a painful place to have a conversation about these things.

You know, these things we hold as true to ourselves, the values or codes that rule our lives.

But still, I continued thinking about the question over the next few minutes, but in reality, it was much longer than a few minutes. At least, that's how it felt. Except for the pain, that was much different in this case.

I'm talking about all my tattoos, you see, and the tattoos represent pain to me because I have so many. I have full sleeves, a full vest, full lowers on my legs, and my back is about 30% done—330 hours or so at this point of tattoo work time.

At the very least, for this event, we're talking $40,000. – $45,000 easy of money that I put into myself, but I, from a technical perspective, pissed away money that I could be living off of right now.

Let's be honest; I still would've fucked around with that money and got myself into my current position. Inevitable.

I think this is because I often feel like the walls are getting closer and closer and closer. It was closing me in, strangling me and my life. It keeps putting me in hopeless positions where some decisions I have to make are a little less appealing.

All of my apathy aside, I wonder, "What will it take to turn things around? What is it that I'm not doing right? How do I keep succeeding at failing at everything I do?" Does it lead me to know where? Or is it putting me right where I'm supposed to be?

What I mean by that is I am curious if I am paying the price for something I did or didn't do, for the actions that I have taken or not taken, and how much more do I have to pay for this, how much more of this shit am I supposed to handle and deal with before I break.

I ask it that way because I feel like I'm being punished. While millions upon millions of people in the United States are suffering like I am, there are untold millions across the planet who are suffering too.

Growing up, I was a big fan of the Punisher comic book by Marvel. Not the movies because they kind of weren't great but yeah. I appreciated his tenacity and determination to make people pay the price for their misdeeds when the system wasn't.

Now while I don't condone his murdering so many people, I do entirely grasp and understand, nay I get it. However, I don't believe I have transgressed in such a manner that the punishment is so intense and relentless in my life.

I recognize that how I feel depends on what is around me and the transpiring events. And that is the same to be said for so many people. But fuck them. Just kidding.

It presents a specter above and beyond what it is now that I am dealing with. Its black cloud brings me pain, suffering, and misery.

I don't feel like I can ever be pleased, and it's not just because of some of the things I have lost in my life, just like everybody else. But not everybody else has mental health issues, and I want to say I'm thankful they don't.

I wonder. I wonder what I did wrong. If you could hear me speaking right now, it would be incredibly somber and self-reflecting or self-reflective. I always want to improve myself, which is a driving factor in my life.

But now I have no drive. I have no desire or push, or motivation to get there. I feel dead inside, and while I'm not scared of this facet, it is a bit concerning because my friends aren't exactly helping me. How could they?

Meanwhile, Good sister is doing a fantastic job of taking care of some financial sides of things. It is challenging to maintain any positivity and maintain my brain.

I mentioned this to Fry a few weeks ago while we were doing technical stuff at his house, and I commented that I was concerned that I was losing my mental acuity and technical skills because I was not using them.

One of the reasons I felt this way was a project that I had started working on was a specific and specialized system build, which had been slowed by parts being delivered that I had ordered off of eBay.

I had ordered a new video card, upgraded processors, a wifi card, and a few other bits in the hopes of building a system that could replace my iMac, the one I'm dictating on right now. Potentially a second system on top of that for downstairs as the video card in the kitchen is just going to shit.

The punishment I'm getting or taking is often related to having to sell or part with things in my life that are part of me, define me and embody who I am.

The paintings, the DAC, the tube amp that I love so much, the diamond engagement ring that my ex-wife gave me back so I could sell it (that lays around my neck). That one hurts a lot. And then my computer. These all represent things that are part of me, and it hurts.

I find myself questioning myself and what I have done; what I did that was so egregious that I'm being punished in such a manner that I feel like I'm falling apart, and I just am having such a fucking hard time dealing with it. The darkness increasingly tears at me.

You know you have issues when you start thinking about or planning how to commit suicide and then work on getting everything in place to carry that out. Or at least you should know!

And the last thing I wanted to do was bring harm to Bugsy, Koni, or Yags.

Another aspect is the consequences of talking openly and honestly with your friends. They either don't want to hear it or are afraid of it because it is tough to deal with that fact.

What I don't understand, and I'm not second-guessing the motives of my friends because I care about them and they are essential to me, and I enjoy them, is that either they're not taking me seriously or they don't know what to do. I don't know what to do.

The only thing I can do is hope that I can find what I did so horrible that I am being punished the way I am or find a way to break out of this. But unfortunately, I don't see either of them being plausible or possible, for that matter, at this time.

I think of what I write on my blog, and often it's just something that comes up in my mind, and I say, oh, that reminds me of this song, and I write a couple of hundred words about it. Then from time to time, I come up with good ideas or ideas and write about them.

This morning I posted a rather lengthy blog about Anesthesia, my absolute favorite song from Type O Negative.

I noted in the first paragraph the following quote "In case you didn't know, Anesthesia from Type O Negative is my favorite song. That includes every Dream Theater song, ever. It holds powerful meanings to me and in my life."

And as I go through, a couple of bits are of interest to help give context to what I'm writing today. And here are a few quotes from my post:

- I fucking feel like everything is surgery now. I feel like parts of me are being destroyed and removed.
- My whole life, my whole world, was destroyed to block the pain, to relieve myself from it. To make me comfortable, comfortable with this horrible shit. I don't feel anything.
- I am fighting the future; I am fighting the past. I cannot win the present.
- I am so broken now that I have dissolved into a mess of alcoholism, drug use, and substance abuse. I am trying to find a way NOT to FEEL ANYTHING! I don't want to feel anything.

If those quotes do not give you enough background or understanding as to how I feel and how it is that I think I have no hope, how I cannot win, then there might not be enough words to do so.

I let those feelings soak in that day. It hurt that I felt so sad and lost. I want to go back to normality, but what is normality?

And just like that, I realized I was so fucking far into my head that I could see myself from afar. Just drifting.

CHAPTER 6 – RELEASE

The paths we walk, the choices we make, how they permeate our lives, and the pain we inflict on ourselves. Ah crap, I can hear some Redemption lyrics from the song "Release" rattling about my head.

> Tired of life and filled with despair and covered with blood from the crosses I bear, but I'm still standing–
> *Redemption, The Fullness of Time: Release.*

I went for a walk the other day. While walking, I spent a reasonable amount of time thinking that I have, slowly but surely, been leaving clues for my inner circle about the stark realities of the decisions I've made and the path I must walk.

Thankfully, I'm thrilled that I'm doing it, as I am setting expectations for myself and my inner circle in the event of the creeping darkness. There'd be no honest way to release me and the burden I feel on my mind.

Yup, I keep hearing that god damn song again echoing in the back of my mind. It's lightly buzzing back there, pushing me to investigate myself further.

I find myself feeling very disappointed in people, and yet I find hope in others where previously there was a void. I've had friends step up and had "friends" that I had to release from my life because they were incapable of being adults.

And I've been saddened by people who cannot maintain a conversation with somebody without getting upset and name-calling. It's just not something people can release themselves from. It's the stark reality of the world that we live in.

That night, I called an old friend whom I've known for over 25 years. While we were talking, I brought up that subject. You know, the one about the darkness that was coming for me. I find it hard to explain at times for the uninitiated.

She's a longtime friend from the short stint where I lived in Florida. At the time we met, I was working for her then-husband. It was Thanksgiving, and he invited me and my roommate "Greg" (I will call him that).

I didn't know that "Greg" and the boss were old friends from their time working for some interwebs dial-up place in the early 1990s. But I knew "Greg" from growing up in the area of NY I was from.

I knew the boss was married, but I knew nothing of her. And to be consistent, we'll call her "Andrea." I'd never met "Andrea" before, so I had no frame of reference.

The boss invited us in, and we were in the dining room, having an adult beverage when this incredibly stunning blonde walked in. I think "Greg" had to help me pick up my jaw after it had dropped.

I didn't gawk for long, but her southern accent was nearly as stunning as her overall beauty. As the night went on, "Andrea" was friendly to me, but not overly. I don't want to piss off the boss.

Friendliness doesn't mean a lap dance, although I would have welcomed it in any other setting. That includes a church, a movie theater, and a cemetery. You get the point.

I believe I've written about her before, elsewhere.

Ok, back to that night. Overall, it was a pleasant time. At the night's end, "Greg" and I thanked our hosts for our goodbyes. I figured I'd never see her again, so it wasn't heartbreaking.

As time passed, she ended up divorcing the boss. I don't recall him giving two shits to have released himself from whatever the deal was.

Because "Andrea" was friends with "Greg," I'd see "Andrea" from time to time when the group would go out to a bar, hang out at someone's apartment, whatever.

"Andrea" was never overly flirtatious with me, but she went through some tough times with the divorce. I'd come to understand that some ten years later.

The last memory of "Andrea" was the last time I saw her while living in Florida. It was like something out of a dream, so surreal that it couldn't have possibly been anything other than a fabrication.

I knew then as I know now; something inside me said it would happen again, inaction grabbing me. Growing up, my father would say, "He who hesitates has lost". So true.

I was with my new roommate, "Terry," who had moved in when my buddy "Greg" moved back to Minnesota to take a job working and doing networking stuff. He had been released from the lease.

That was painful as I had moved there because of my friendship with "Greg." But, even today, I don't hold it against "Greg" for doing what was best for him.

"Terry" was excellent and from the same general area as "Greg" and myself. However, he was younger than us, so I had not met him until moving to Florida.

"Terry" was a part of the crew that would hang out together on the weekends before "Greg's" departure after being released from the lease. So he got "Terry" to step into that spot.

Over the next few months, his girlfriend (whom I called "girlfriend," complete with a lowercase g) moved in. She was a nice gal, with one slight side note.

She had dated "Greg" for a few months. It was weird to see her there. She was kind of like furniture.

Well, there's a second note there. Seeing her walk around naked while being "Greg's" furniture and not caring was weird. And the same thing when she was "Terry's" furniture and had the same attitude.

She was friendly, and I can't fault her for being an exhibitionist. But, on the other hand, I'm sure she felt as if she had released part of herself to be able to do that.

And she liked Montana quite a bit. Then again, who didn't? He was a super rad red Maine Coon, a life companion through and through.

Sorry about that; back to the story about "Andrea."

I was standing there, trying not to stare at a spectacular woman that I had thought about from time to time.

What was she like to fall asleep with? Did she prefer holding hands with the left or the right? You know, stuff.

As the conversation about whom the fuck knows what concluded, not paying attention as I wasn't a part of it, I watched as she turned and walked away from me.

Sashaying her ass as if to say, "Hey, look at me! I'm something you can't have.". Either that or telling me she loved anal. Shrug.

A few years ago, I had another one of those moments with someone I was too shy or scared to ask out. And I watched the girl from the grocery store walk away, just as I had watched "Andrea."

Shit, I'm in the weeds again.

Somehow, we have managed to stay in touch for many years now. I have promised "Andrea" a kiss, just a kiss, probably sometime in the last 25 years. Lol.

I don't recall this promise, but I have faith in her, to be honest, nor would I suggest that she should or could release me from that agreement.

"Andrea" and I talked the other night, and I mentioned to her that I had been looking at airfare as I needed to fulfill my commitment to her, even if it was the last thing I did or the last bit of money that I had.

At first, I believe she was taken aback by my willingness to openly and honestly communicate, how much value I place on my integrity above so much else, and its importance in my life.

I know there's a chapter in one of my unreleased books about integrity—something about a code or some shit.

I think it's hard for people to understand a good human and the sheer amount of work that goes into being good. There's an immense amount of effort to it.

You have to be willing to stand up for yourself, and you have to be willing to stand up for others. You have to be ready to walk the walk. Who are you, and what do you want to be?

Very importantly, you have to be able to admit when you're wrong and not because you're being backed in a corner. So release yourself of that burden and free yourself of that pain.

Because you're a good human, you will always know the difference between right and wrong.

I find that it is the respect you show somebody to listen to what they say and recognize your wrongdoing. Then, you will be released from their doubt and strengthen that bond.

While we typically don't want to admit to being wrong, that is a human condition; doing this is essential to your integrity.

Without integrity, you are just a shell of a person and more apt to be a piece of shit than a stand-up human. Again, you must release yourself to achieve this level of integrity.

For as long as I can remember, I have tried to walk the walk. I have wanted to be an adult and keep my feelings in check; although in private, that's another story.

But it's important because people are lunatics and unhinged. They come at you with anger, spite, and vitriol and expect you to do the same. So you have integrity when you do not retaliate, and you listen. You listen.

Sigh, again, dude? Ok, back on track as I tend to get into the weeds.

I have known "Andrea" for 25 years and have repeatedly acknowledged that I am responsible for fulfilling my obligation. Therefore, I think she could understand why it was important to me.

Don't get me wrong; I don't want to fly anywhere, let alone to Chicago again. But I'm going to do that because I am a man. I am a man of my word. That is integrity.

They are doing things you don't want to do for the sake of doing them because they are right.

There is a line that one must walk and save yourself. To be the human you are supposed to be, you have to own your own shit. If you can't, you are weak.

Do you lack the courage and strength to stand in the face of anger?

You would think I would have something more to say about integrity right now for the amount of stuff I've written about integrity. But the truth is, I can talk about it all I want, but in the end, I have to go to Chicago to fulfill a promise.

Ya gotta do what you gotta do, right?

But seriously, I had every intention to do that, even if it's the last thing I do. Good and longtime friends are hard to come by, even harder to hold.

And that's the great thing about having integrity. Your friends know that they can count on you.

If you can maintain those values, the people around you will always know they can count on you. And they all know where you stand on something and how important it is to your moral fabric to maintain that.

CHAPTER 7 – FAITH & DARKNESS

Faith continues to be an epic struggle for all of Man; otherwise, darkness creeps upon you, calling your name and misspelling it. Fucking clowns. Like the movie "IT," but dumber.

I was talking with a former associate the other day. He insulted me and demeaned my feelings about having lost something significant to me.

He ridiculed me so that I would have stabbed him in the throat with my dick if I were a violent person. But I didn't. Nor would I ever. And not just because I'm insecure about my cock.

I allowed this to continue for a while, not just one conversation but many more over a solid piece of time. It was always a test of faith, even if I was not religious.

As the days slipped into weeks, I ignored this person because I had faith in myself. I had faith that I was strong enough to take anything he could try to throw at me. And one day, I finally had had enough, and I told him.

"It does not matter what you think. It does not matter what you say. You are inconsequential. You are insignificant. And I'd like to remind you of the age-old saying, "sticks and stones may break my bones, but names will never hurt me."

I had the opportunity to work for CNIPROC.LIVE, and what I would do would be ethically against my morals and fabric.

It would be against my values, but I was in such a position that I had to take the job. It was taking the job or killing myself. Literally, and there's the darkness again.

I worked there for a while, and every day I said to myself, "I'm going to quit soon because this is not right. This is immoral." Eventually, I was ushered out via downsizing, like so many others.

They didn't give me any hope or faith; they kept me away from that darkness. But then, I lost it all. The job and money. Everything. And I was very angry, confused, and frustrated.

What have I done to have been put into a position like this?

What part of the Karma universe did I shit on to get treated in such a horrible manner? What did I do wrong? And I had no answers like asking Bugsy, Koni, or Yags how their dinner was.

Then, something remarkable occurred to me. I had some stocks from <u>CNIPROC.LIVE</u>, and they were doing pretty well—more than pretty well.

The point where I made money hand over fist over fist, and I could see the cashout, or at least I thought it was a cashout. I had to have faith in that coming to fruition.

But the money, the money kept pulling on me. I could have better toys, I could have better spaces, and I could have better access to people and resources. And you know what that stuff does?

It questions your faith and positions the darkness to rule over you, suffocating your existence.

There was a rather significant and negative downside here. Having that money brought access to drugs. And oh boy, the drugs. Someday I'll talk about that, but know it was fun.

But then <u>CNIPROC.LIVE</u> had a massive scandal, and its stock tanked. That money went "poof." My benefits are gone. Health Insurance was relegated to using the ACA (Obamacare).

What a fucking shit fuck that is. This doctor is covered; this doctor says no fucking way. I'm sure people understand this one.

I needed a particular drug for my thyroid, and dealing with the side effects was difficult. I had no job; I had no insurance; I was living off selling some of the stocks from time to time.

While all that was great, getting that medication was very challenging. I saw my doctor, who said they couldn't give me the medicines unless I submitted myself to a battery of tests.

I said, "Are you fucking kidding me? How much do these tests cost?"

The response was predictable. "Since you don't have insurance, at least $1,000."

And I stopped. And I wondered to myself again, what the fuck is going on? Is this that slap from Karma?

I felt like the walls were closing in again, and I couldn't take it. My life was being battered and destroyed. I turned to the darkness. No, my desperation caught hold of me.

I made an appointment with my vet and brought
Bugsy in a few weeks earlier than was scheduled. I'd
been with my vet for 13 years, between several
clinics. I was so happy and proud when he opened up
his clinic.

He was stunned that I was in and asked about that. I
told him about my issue, needing thyroid medication.

I asked him if he would prescribe the non-addictive,
no psychotropic or hallucinogenic, or euphoric
feeling thyroid medication to the cat in this specific
dosage I needed.

He said no. He said no because that was immoral and
ethically wrong. So I didn't argue with him, I
understood, and I knew it was a big ask.

I thanked him for at least discussing with me and said
I would see him at Bugsy's next appointment a few
weeks later.

And to be honest, all of the subsequent times that I
saw him, we never talked about it. He never
mistreated me and was always so kind and generous
to me.

A couple of weeks later, I found myself in the same
situation as I was before. Again, I am afraid of what's
happening or what could happen even though I've
requested assistance.

This time I had asked for assistance from the State of Arizona and the United States Federal Government, and with all of their programs, I was getting nowhere.

I had my Obamacare insurance come up for renewal, and as I was filling out the form, I could only enter the amount of money I was making as my unemployment insurance. I get to the end of the document, and it says

"Too bad, so sad, you don't make enough money; why don't you try something else because you are a giant loser?"

Hyperbole. OK, that's not really what it said, but it did indicate that I wasn't making enough money on unemployment to be a part of the Obamacare program, and it did suggest looking into alternatives.

Medicaid and Medicare are a joke. Which is all great and everything, except none of my doctors accept it. Lovely.

What exactly was I supposed to do when I was in a position like this? I had no one to help me, and nothing pointed in the right direction. I don't understand why I am just spinning my wheels and getting nowhere.

It is incredibly discouraging and somewhat frustrating to be in this position.

And the darkness leaped back into my life, filling cracks in my brain like pouring paint made of some super sticky syrup all over a table.

It never feels like it goes away. It lurks in the depth of my mind every once and a while, knocking at the front door as if to remind me it was there. This darkness never asked me for anything. It just wanted everything.

But I knew it was there. I kept trying to push it away, make it stop. I tried alcohol. I tried marijuana. I tried a variety of prescribed medications. I tried other fun drugs.

The darkness was always there, waiting for me and for me to make a mistake. To backslide. To admit defeat. To allow it to take over and consume my soul, my essence.

I feel like the darkness keeps calling me, subconsciously at the very least. It is an ever-present pulsing beacon. I can hear it like a counter in the recesses of my brain like it's beating a lobe to kingdom come.

The darkness's everything you think it would be. It never stops. It will never stop; it knows no way other than to be the bringer of pain. It's an unfortunate way to think about it.

The darkness will always be calling to me.

For as long as I have remembered, the darkness has haunted me for as long as I have been. It has always been the doubt that clouds my mind. It has always been the anxiety that has punished me.

The darkness is a cloud that brings nothingness. It brings self-desolation and despair. It is all that destroys life. It is all that cripples your mind, preventing you from any happiness.

It is doom. It is sadness incarnate. It is limitless. It does not know time.

Many people relate this feeling to "goth" stuff. However, I can assure you that for myself, at the very least, "goth" wasn't the initiator of this. No, not at all.

Having not knowingly listened to "goth" until the first time I heard Type O Negative (Christian Woman) circa 1994. I don't think I'd ever heard "goth." The whole genre gets a bit of a bad rap.

I have always had this sorrow inside of me. It is
always there; it never goes away. It is ever-present.
It's ever crippling. It's the bringer of doom more than
anything else.

There are times when, much like my knee pain, I
have wished that there was something that I could
give of myself to make it go away. But then I end up
sitting in the shower with the shower head spraying
down my knees.

Nothing makes that pain go away. Nothing makes my
knees not hurt. I've had six knee surgeries, yet I still
am nearly always in pain.

I'm always catering to my knees, those fucks. The
pain makes me want to do much harm to myself. I
often live my life around them. Around how I know
they are going to feel "later."

CHAPTER 8 – PAIN & POWER

How is the world against me? How is nothing going my way? Just like everyone else is experiencing. The power of being in pain and the power of pain ruling your life.

I have faith in the power of my mind. And then, I started to see the cracks in the wall. I might as well have been listening to Pink Floyd's The Wall.

I started losing my faith in myself and looking at the darker side of things. It's the dark side of my soul, the dark side of my brain.

When I started doing that, it was during the pandemic.

It was just me; I had no support. I had nobody to help give me strength. I have nothing, nada, zero, zilch, zip. I could feel the darkness pulling on me. I could hear it, feel it, calling my name.

That was the first time I recall hearing it, telling me there's no way out. There's not going to be anybody to save me.

No matter how hard I try, no one will help me. I accepted that, and so I started to deal with it. And I kept losing my faith. That fucking pull was so powerful.

I kept losing my faith in myself and started measuring everything I would have to do to have in place if I was to get hurt. Get hurt in any way, whether by acting out or hurting myself.

And I wanted to hurt myself in a large and significant way. So that was my go-to when I was sad, angry, or happy. It was one of my three safe places. But that's not important to this story.

I couldn't get tattooed because I'm not working, have no money, and tattoos aren't free. So far as I know, "The Shaman" charges me every time I have a session.

I believe I could steer myself clear, and good things would happen. But they weren't, and the darkness just kept coming.

I started looking at the calendar and thought, "If this isn't resolved in my life by this point, then I'm going to have no alternative."

As I said earlier, I will not leave Bugsy, Yags, and Koni. They are my gatos.

75

The power of my strength, the power of my faith, comes from hope. And Bugsy, Yags, and Koni give me hope; they give me something to live for; I probably would've killed myself a long time ago.

And there is some more of the darkness seeping out.

And then I started thinking about it. But yet, I could feel my faith slipping away over and over. What are you supposed to do when you have no faith?

The pain was so powerful that it was almost static cling, and I had no dryer sheets to help repel it, let alone delint my fur-filled clothes. And then it happened.

I was in the kitchen the other day working on a blog post, and suddenly I felt my right knee pop. And a second time. Wait, three's the magic number.

I've had four surgeries on that knee, three of which were scopes. Those were in 2006, 2007, and 2010. In 2016, I had ACL + microfracture surgery on that knee.

Not that the left side is any better, I've only had two scopes on it, 2006 and 2016.

This event couldn't have happened at a worse time. Here I am, out of work, incredibly broken in my heart, soul, and mind. It is one of the last things I need to be a problem with.

As I stood in the kitchen, grasping my knee, I thought, "Well, 2020 is fucking me again. It keeps finding new and innovative ways to do it, that's for fucking sure."

After digesting that statement, I remembered coming back from Minnesota in 2016 and thinking about it in a much broader and stronger context.

I was in Minnesota in 2016 because my most excellent sisters wanted me to be back for my mother's funeral. I didn't want to go as I did not believe then, and still now, that she deserved my presence.

There was much speculation on whether I would undergo two more knee surgeries. The right knee had decided to do the **three-pop shuffle** and make me miserable.

When I got back, I looked for my orthopedist's number to get that shit setup. I trusted him because he had done four of my previous knee surgeries.

Come to find out that he had either passed away or shut down his practice; everything was boarded up, and the phone lines busied out.

Back to the ice packs, trying to get the swelling down and relieve some of the tightness. It was uncomfortable, and the amount of swelling made my tattoos look fat.

My boss at that time, very much so the best boss that I had ever had, suggested a place that did his pectoral surgery. I was hesitant at first as I could be adverse to change.

I saw the orthopedist, who confirmed precisely what I had suspected after some x-rays and a pair of MRIs. Nothing good.

There was another tear in the meniscus of my left knee, and the ACL in my right knee was, well, not exactly there anymore. I suppose that's what happens when you first tear it in 1988.

We started to formulate a plan, and of course, these types of projects take a while.

One has to consider having multiple surgeries in particular proximity as being under too many times is not very desirable.

One funny thing that transpired between the two surgeries was that I was contacted by the owner of the house I was renting. She informed me that she wanted it back, and adorably and positively, she explained the reasoning to me.

It made complete sense to me, and I agreed it was the right decision for all parties involved. When I brought up the timing, she told me I would have six weeks to move out.

It was about when I mentioned to her that I was having ACL surgery in less than a month and that I had the left knee scoped two weeks before this phone call.

So now I have to move my home in a particular window of time that fell between the two knee surgeries. So hopefully, you see the difficulties in what I am getting at.

While I did pull this off successfully, it was because I found a house roughly 312 feet up the street. I loved the new place, and I was able to move in tiny stages.

I could come home from work, pack up some plastic bins, load them into the car, drive to the new place, and unpack. That meant I did not have to deal with bullshit in any room. At all.

I could go at my own pace, and when moving day came, I had professional movers handle the furniture because I physically could not.

I just was too broken, physically and mentally.

I had completed my move and settled for about a week; my good sister came out from CT to help me for the first few days after my ACL surgery. That was very kind of her, and I will always appreciate that.

She knows this, and she is a wonderful person. I'm fortunate for the values our parents taught us, my two sisters and me. I know I can trust them implicitly.

I know they will never harm me, be it physically, emotionally, mentally, or financially, and they both know the same about each other and myself.

Everything with the surgery went well, and I'm thankful I had her to assist me. She helped regulate pain medication and ensured that I followed the rules.

I'm bringing this up because it's essential to understand that while my sisters and I are all spread out, there is an underlying core component to our fundamental values and value system.

We are always willing to do something for each other. And in this case, it was the willingness of my oldest sister to help me out that made all the difference in the world.

The one main thing rattling through my head was back in 2016. The orthopedist and insurance company were fighting over prices. I was getting all of these packets in the mail, including price breakdowns and specifications, what they were willing to pay, and whatnot.

And the scope for my left knee was quoted at $60,000. That is correct, six-zero-comma-zero-zero-zero. I was stunned when I saw those, and I even brought them to work to have some of my colleagues review them to see if I was out of my gourd.

I know my orthopedist does not take Obamacare. Apparently, he doesn't take blowjobs as payment, either. What is this world coming to?

All jokes aside, I don't have the cash to do any procedures, whether an MRI, an x-ray, or an office visit. I just spent $120, which broke my soul when I had to see my primary care to get a refill on a script.

CHAPTER 9 – PAIN

While I have lived many lifetimes with knee problems, it sucks, and I thought I was done with it in 2016. It just keeps getting worse as a reoccurring payment of pain.

It's not enough to be running low on money and not having a job, to not have anywhere to go to do anything, but then I have the looming specter of a potentially disastrous scenario.

It's always looming. More pain, please. Just never-ending pain. More and more and more pain. Fuck!

As you can imagine, it profoundly impacts your life when you are not mobile. For example, I can't exercise because of the pressure it puts on them, and living in a two-story house has been trying while dealing with my knee pain.

That pisses me off even more.

What do I need to do to get back on track? Why does it seem like I'm getting shit on at every turn?

I was chatting with an old friend the other night, and we were talking about the world's current condition, and what ostensibly would happen if society continued in the shit show direction it was going.

I reminded them that a fixed, extended, or extensive lockdown of 4 to 6 weeks would be the end for me.

I wouldn't be able to survive it, and there's nobody who's going to be able to. So more jobs are lost if we have an imposed lockdown, and I don't see my recovery ability.

I'm going to be a statistic, and while that is very scary and surreal, I've been preparing myself for this for a long time.

I have repeatedly articulated that to several intricately involved people in my life. But, in contrast, I don't always expect people to understand my feelings or decisions.

I hope that those close to me can see a consistent behavior of open and honest conversations while preparing people for the future.

I am talking about specific taboo or complex topics, things that come from the darkness, and the pain it brings. The pain calls for it.

Ask them if they voted for this person or believe in this social construct issue. No, not Apple shit; this is about death, the people around you who do not want you to die per se.

I think it isn't effortless. It's a difficult conversation for people to have, and it takes an influential person to be able to be open and honest about it.

It takes a particular type of makeup not only to disseminate the information but also to receive it.

I know that if I had a friend who expressed to me that they were suffering through an extended bout of depression, I would reach my hand out to them. But the last thing I want is to be saying again something I said in the past...

To Quote Redemption, **Sapphire:**

"I feel like I'm drowning, And everywhere I turn, the water's deeper."

And that's what it feels like. And it's nobody's fault, but it's entirely my own. I had made this mess based on my decisions throughout my life, and I only have myself to blame. So I own my own shit.

If I were to fail, it would be my fault. I cannot blame anybody for myself. This is my pain, the pain that brings on the darkness.

That's something that people can learn a lot from, and I wish there were a teaching seminar class about owning your own shit that was a part of our high school education curriculum.

How amazing would it be to have come out of high school, whether you went to college or not, and known that whatever problems you have are yours, and if you let other people make your problems worse, you need to fix that?

My problems right now are my doing, and I own that. PROC LIVE is just a symptom of a systemic collapse of ethics and morality cascading into the crevices like an oil spill; it just coats everything.

It destroys and suffocates everything in its path. For example, look at some old environmental videos of the Exxon Valdes and when they ran ashore.

Sorry, that was a little bit of the sidebar. PROC.LIVE is the bringer of doom. They are the evil you can't believe exists, except you know it exists because of the structure of our society.

How people are not as well-regarded as they should be in the name of the Almighty Dollar.

Companies don't care about you; they don't give a shit about you. Not only that, but they were terrible people. Not evil on their own, but just wrong. And when you put a grouping of solid influence or high-powered bad people together, that is where evil comes from

I wish that I cared. I wish I had given a shit about anything other than Bugsy, Yags, Koni, and myself.

Throughout my writings, I have mentioned how important they are to me, how important my gatos are, and that I did not exist for a long time without them.

And when I say things like that to my friends, they either tell me they don't want to talk about it or stop talking about it because it's upsetting.

But the reality is that if you care, I do not have a problem or issue or concern or lack of anything or nothing negative to say about my friends when you're not happy about it.

Not everybody can have profound and dark conversations with another person, whether exposing themselves or listening to somebody's pain.

You have to care about discussing yourself in a very raw, open, honest, and caring manner. You have to be able to talk about pain cogently.

Having a conversation is very important, and I think it's something that has gotten lost along the way. I learned a couple of outstanding human lessons between 2015 and 2018.

Both lessons were around not caring about what people thought about you and owning up to your mistakes, committing, and being willing to have a conversation about either or both.

There is not much somebody will say to me that has not been said before or that would be not very kind. I live a libertarian philosophical lifestyle.

The general rule to this philosophy, which I believe I covered earlier, is I don't care what the fuck you are doing so long as it doesn't impact me and doesn't affect children, the elderly, or animals, and it is within the purview of the law.

It's a great release; I'm not a Karen, and I don't have to worry about that because I don't care. I will follow the rules, and unless somebody else doesn't, I don't care unless it hits one of those last categories. I don't care.

Maybe I have shed myself of responsibility by turning myself into some apathetic hermit. But ultimately, I do not feel that that's the case, but the idea has some merit.

I pride myself on conversing with people, not getting roiled up, and telling him to stick his head in a bucket of water and take a deep breath. But unfortunately, I'm not that person, and I have never been that person for the most part.

And I'm thankful for that because it is much easier to make my life.

I think people can learn a lot from philosophical change where you stop being so obsessive-compulsive or outright hateful to what other people are doing and focus more on positively releasing yourself from being bound to societal norms that suggest that if you vote R or if you vote D then your perspectives of society are entirely different and therefore none congruent.

The failure to have an adult conversation with another human and not be capable of handling yourself calmly and rationally is an incredibly damming indignation of our cultural institutions that preach that there is no longer that ability between humans.

I find it hard to believe. I find it morally reprehensible that we would promote a cultural standard of tribal partisanship, knowing what that does to the overall collective psyche.

A culture that can't communicate is destined and bound to fail. This is because there is no reasonable way in which you should know what somebody else is doing if they don't tell you.

This is especially true with turn signals. I'll leave the rest of that pain in the ass shit for another day.

The point of writing today is that I worry about myself but have complete confidence that I can execute my directives if necessary.

And I know I will have planned legally and socially if anything goes wrong, like the darkness overcoming all of the pain.

CHAPTER 10 – APATHY CREATES DESPAIR

I have been fighting with general malaise and a crashing and overwhelming wave of apathy. It's made me feel like nothing matters, and I don't care about anything anymore.

I don't want to sound like I'm giving up, but rather that I am so broken down and spent that I can no longer function as an adult in many ways.

Now hear me out. I'm saying that being an adult is all about decision-making and the capability of good decision-making.

I have been having a hard time with that, and I feel that no matter what I have done, it just doesn't matter. Nothing I do helps me move forward.

I have five months now of being unemployed. I've gone through all of my savings. I've sold off a number of my possessions. I have borrowed money I don't know I'll ever be able to pay back.

And now I'm standing at the precipice of an even more significant failure because I have to sell some of the most important things to me, not the gatos, which hurts a lot.

It may be that a level of pain is necessary to grow as a human, but I have stopped caring about that. I feel like my decisions are poor, and I have no one to turn to to help me.

And before you say it, every decision and everything that has happened to me is of my volition, and I own that. That is an adult statement, but it's the decision-making.

It's the drinking for me. I have a huge problem, and while I am not violent or competitive when I drink heavily, it's the fact that I'm doing that.

It is not suitable for me to subject myself to a self-inflicted line of torture.

Today is December 11, and with the holidays coming up, I find myself in a position where I don't know how to make any of that work.

I have had many personal problems, issues, traumas, or whatever in 10 days. It might be 11 days. I would have to check it, and I don't fucking feel like it. Christmas was complicated because of my father's surgery on December 26, 1993.

In August 1993, my father was diagnosed with a brain aneurysm, and they decided that surgery was the best course of action.

That was our last Christmas because my father suffered a rather massive stroke during the surgery. Good sister was there, as was Bad sister.

For note, Bad sister is not evil; she's never done anything to harm me, physically, emotionally, or financially. I coined the term good and bad sisters to quickly and easily identify them with my friends or acquaintances.

I am blessed to have the two of them in my life, and the level of trust between us is fantastic. That reminds me of a story from many years ago.

After my maternal grandmother passed away, the three of us went through our parents' house and identified the things we wanted down the road after they passed. All three of us were calling out what we wanted so that our parents were both aware, and the three of us knew what the others wanted.

As my sisters were going through jewelry in our parents' room, I was in the dining room with our mother and father, and they asked what it was that I would want, and I told them the dining room set and the china that our father's mother gave to them as a wedding gift.

I would get that dining room set and china when I bought my first house in 2000. I wasn't expecting it, but my parents had it. I trucked it to my house. It was a very kind gesture.

As we were standing there, I turned to my mother, and she said, "You only have two sisters, and you will only ever have two sisters. They are your only family." And it blew me away and solidified part of the values my parents had brought to us, to Good and Bad sister.

Back to my father... That stroke paralyzed him on his dominant right side and scrambled his brain sufficiently so he could no longer care for himself.

That burden, generally speaking, fell onto my mother and, well, another story.

In my mind, I associate Christmas with my father's surgery. Christmas of 1993 was the last one we had as a family, which was difficult.

When that's ripped away from you of no wrongdoing on your part, it really sucks, and generally speaking, I'm not alone in this world to feel that way.

The only saving grace for this event, for losing my father, as I have always believed to be an accurate representation, is what made me decide I wanted to leave Minnesota.

It is the catalyst for that change.

Four months after his surgery, in April 1994, I came out to Arizona to explore and check things out, and I was able to stay with a friend of my father's in Cave Creek, Arizona.

Cave Creek is roughly 20 minutes, 25 minutes north of where I live in North Phoenix, and it was terrific. The sun, the blue skies, the temperatures.

A few days before I came out to Arizona for that visit in April 1994, we had a blizzard in Minnesota for which we got roughly 2 feet of snow, if I recall correctly.

And since my mother was too cheap to buy a snowblower, I got to shovel the driveway, three cars wide and five vehicles deep.

I realized just how much I fucking hated the snow and how much I fucking hated being in Minnesota. I knew I was never going to get anywhere there.

I've mentioned this before, but in the late 80s into the early 90s, CNIPROC.LIVE had done its first-ever widescale downsizing and laid off roughly 25 or 30,000 people.

And Minnesota was pretty much CNIPROC.LIVE country.

At some point in your life, you would have worked for CNIPROC.LIVE or somebody in your family would have. In my case, my father had, my mother was downsized, and both sisters were downsized.

Down the road, 12 or 13 years later, I was downsized from CNIPROC.LIVE while working at/or for Federally Expresso.

When people with Masters degrees in engineering or PHDs in molecular science compete for jobs at Home Depot, there's no forward growth here.

As a result, there is no investment into the community that will solve the problem of a surplus of people and an ever-decreasing job market.

I saw it then, I could see what was happening or what would happen, but I could not comprehend it.

So it's one of those things where a little bit later on, you can better understand what you saw based on having more life experience.

I knew that I would never get anywhere in Minnesota because of things like this, and as I flew into Phoenix, I was blown away by the reflecting mountains in Arizona.

Most people don't know this, but Arizona is a mountainous state. Even here in Phoenix, the Valley of the Sun, there are tons of mountains regularly packed with hikers within Phoenix.

A lot of great trails and some excellent weather for the vast majority of the year.

So here I am. I went to the car rental location and got my car. I started driving, and I saw the temperature outside was 94°.

That morning in Minnesota, it was like 40°, and now I am in a bright, beautiful sunny fantastic environment, and it's hot.

But it wasn't the Minnesota 94° that killed half of the population.

No, this was the proverbial dry heat. When there is no moisture in the air, it feels more like an oven than a swamp. Probably where they get swamp ass from.

It hit 100° in the middle of April during my five-day stay. I had never thought I would ever experience something like that, and a year and a half later, at the end of July 1995, it hit 121° in Phoenix.

You have no idea how hot that is because your body can't do anything. You don't sweat because it evaporates almost instantly; you don't know you are overheating.

Instead, it would help if you were drinking infinite amounts of water.

As a further note on the temperature, I have lived here in Phoenix for 26 years, and I have experienced 121°, 120°, and 119° many times. The summer of 2020 was the strangest.

There it is! Phoenix has experienced its 144th day this year with a high temperature of 100°F or greater, reaching 100°F at 2:37 PM MST this afternoon.

This beats the previous record of 143 days set in 1989. #azwx pic.twitter.com/UbKLHSnw6e— NWS Phoenix (@NWSPhoenix) October 14, 2020

Please take a second and read that again. We experienced **144 days of temperatures greater than 100° in 2020.** That is insane. And as I've grown older, it pisses me off increasingly every year.

Yet I can't imagine living somewhere that has seasons or snow.

<u>Washington Post</u> article highlights:

The overall 2020 heat records in Phoenix are too many to list.

But among the more notable are new highs for the number of days at or above 110°(53) and 115°(14).

Not to mention, Phoenix never dropped below 90°for for a record 28-night stretch during the summer.

I'm asking you to reread that quote because it's insane. I have no words. But this is 2020, the most screwed up, destructive, and fucked up year.

Now that feels like we're in the simulation. But that's off-topic.

CHAPTER 11 – ANGER

Whenever I think about anger and destruction, I think about the term Democide. It's not something many people know about or understand until the basic constructs are explained to them.

https://www.hawaii.edu/powerkills/MURDER.HTM and https://www.hawaii.edu/powerkills/20TH.HTM

Democide is a term proposed by R. J. Rummel since at least 1994[1], who defined it as "the intentional killing of an unarmed or disarmed person by government agents acting in their authoritative capacity and pursuant to government policy or high command".[2] According to him, this definition covers a wide range of deaths, including forced labor and concentration camp victims; killings by "unofficial" private groups; extrajudicial summary killings; and mass deaths due to governmental acts of criminal omission and neglect, such as in deliberate famines, as well as killings by de facto governments, i.e. civil war killings.[2] This definition covers any murder of any number of persons by any government.[2]

People seemingly fail to remember that aggressive dictators, communists, fascists, socialists, authoritarians, and assholes are responsible for unfathomable atrocities.

It blows my mind that idiot children today aren't taught an ounce of shit because sympathizers of these ideologies run our schools.

They believe that power is not having any debate or allowing opponents. That power is derived from the barrel of a gun they do not want their citizens to have for fear of them rising against them.

They purport that oppression from your government is better than freedom from it. That these forms of government were better than the United States of America.

I'd like to remind you that The United States of America is the greatest nation in the history of this planet. Period.

I find it insane that people do not understand or have never been exposed to this concept.

People don't remember that approximately 260 million people were murdered by their governments in the 20th century.

By their government.

It's sickening. No, maddening. I cannot comprehend how as a society that this is not a central part of our core curriculum of the educational syllabus during the 20th century.

I cannot comprehend how anybody could justify it being okay to murder people! Not even just one. How could you not be pissed off and angry over that?

Think about this for a second, 260 million souls. Two hundred sixty million souls were lost.

They could have been the next Einstein, helped us understand warp drive technology, or perhaps somebody who would have cured cancer.

The sheer amount of possibilities is staggering, yet the average college jackass doesn't know about a goddamn thing that their much-beloved Soviet Union did.

Yup. The Soviet Union was complicit and responsible for the murder of almost 62 million people. 62 million people. That, my friends, is Democide.

To murder 260 million people is roughly equivalent to murdering every person in the United States that doesn't live in California or Texas. Every fucking person.

It's not like this is even a partisan issue. The lives of the people murdered in Democide all mattered, yet nobody cared.

It just makes me sick. So many hypocrites and two-faced clowns who only care about themselves and how they can enrich themselves over anybody else.

There is no compassion; there is just power and money. There's no compassion…. That's just so sad. That's CNIPROC.LIVE. Fuck them; I can't contain that anger.

I grew further concerned about my health and well-being with everything going on.

From time to time, I would make macabre jokes with my friends in hopes that they could understand the coming inevitability. And, of course, they'd be angry at me over the fact.

I wish I had a better term for it, but the reality is that I will not leave my gatos, and I will not be homeless.

Over the years, I have accumulated a certain amount of supplies; we were panicking back when the Ebola outbreak was happening in Africa.

I had picked up a roll of 200-foot, 6- or 8-mm thick of StuffemFull plastic. We would refer to it as part of my Dexter equipment.

Sadly, I am not interested in harming other people and do not have the necessary knives or saws.

I had this enormous amount of plastic sheeting and plenty of duct tape. Please bear with me if you can see where I'm going with this.

One day I was in the third car garage, looking for a box to ship something, and it dawned on me that instead of using the two-car garage attached to the house, why not just use the third-car garage?

Here's the darkness coming in; I used a tape measure to figure out how much sheeting I needed to cover the overhead garage door and window.

I then wondered if I should use the plethora of StuffEmFull garbage bags I have, which I had gotten over the years.

They are instrumental as blackout curtains do not show any light coming from a particular location. This is great when no power and a fiasco are happening worldwide.

As I stood in the garage, having just measured how much tape and plastic sheeting I needed to close it off, I thought about that.

I certainly feel the world's light is getting very dark, not even growing but straight up very close. I thought to myself, am I not a good man? Can I fight against the evil that men do?

As I continued to stand there, I kept thinking about the quote. But I've been beaten down so much, for so long, that I questioned heavily whether or not I was a good man.

Was I still a good person? What had I done that was so horrible?

Or is it because of something I will do that is horrible? Something that is incredibly dark and will land me in a place that I am prepared to go to because that's my option. It's also my decision.

I looked around a little more and considered what I would need to move out of this third garage, which is detached, into the main garage to back my car into it.

And then I thought, do I back in, or do I go nose-first? And that is a question that is best asked while on a VPN.

I will not plug a VPN provider here, but you should predominately use one because, inevitably, that information will get into the hands that will seek to use it against you later.

CHAPTER 12 – DISILLUSION

Disillusion: to realize that a belief or an idea is false. The pain that brings the darkness to me, handing my soul over.

The other day, I was sitting in the park trying to relax from the stress of what had become of us, become of me. I noticed a crowd gathering around a Man, perhaps 50 yards away. It was odd that I hadn't seen this as I sat down.

The Man was gesturing wildly, but the crowd looked intently as they appeared to be absorbing his words.

I turned towards the small crowd and started listening, albeit passively. I stopped focusing on what was happening around me, letting myself absorb the scene. At first, I couldn't understand what I was listening to.

But as time passed and the more the Man spoke, the more I recognized the words. They were captivating, but something was off. Very off.

It's as if I had heard all of this before, but I'd not been aware. Déjà Vu, perhaps? Did I read it somewhere on the interwebs? I couldn't put my finger on it. Nevertheless, it bothered me, so I crept closer to hear his thoughts.

The Man spoke about a wide range of topics, which seemed random, yet his points were captivating, to the point where I could see the bulbs turn on for those who were skeptical but then became disillusioned with the topics.

Disillusion… Where'd that come from? I don't recall using the phrase in some time… disillusioned, hmmm.

What I remembered first was the Man talking about "the system." On and on about it, but I knew how I felt about it. Even now, I could feel myself getting warmer.

"It is a system used as a propaganda machine to enslave the mind and destroy our souls. Corporations lie, deceive, and pander to those they can make money off of. They continue to spew propaganda and disinformation to control us like puppets."

I thought, "Is the Man in the park talking about CNIPROC. LIVE? He must be…"

Another I heard from the Man: "Our masters continue to deny the actions that they continue, as their oppression rules our lives, half-truths, and gossip, the truth we shall never see. This is because they manipulated our minds.

This is part of our daily lives. No one can say that it is not. No one can say that it's not their fault. It's all of our faults. We have allowed it to come to this, and we will continue to enable it."

This touched me in an intensely emotional way.

"With our futures in their hands, are we presumptuous to believe that our society is in decline?

How can we allow ourselves to be so blind? The Companies fear us, and this causes them to hold us down. They work to discredit and destroy anyone who stands in their way.

For how much longer are we going to allow this to continue? Why have we allowed these corporate conglomerates to control us through their propaganda? Why are we not protesting with our feet and our wallets?

"We should be boycotting these corporate conglomerates that cater to the rich and powerful. They have taken the American Dream from us and turned us into mindless drones."

My mind wandered about, all the while hearing, "…losing ourselves to them and never gaining a damn thing.

"We need to wake the F up and realize that we are being destroyed mentally, psychologically, and most importantly, spiritually.

"We need everyone to yell out, 'Wake Up!'. We need to give everyone a voice. Yes, everyone. We can't allow our movement to be biased upon color, creed, or sexual orientation.

"Because it is these people who need it the most. You, the people. People like you!" He pointed randomly. "What we are doing is counterproductive. That is what the Corporations want.

"They are happy in their own lives. The problem is that the rich and powerful want to stay that way and do anything to keep it.

"We need to rise from the ashes of our society and tell them we will not allow this anymore. That is what our beloved country was founded upon.

"And somewhere, we went wrong. **WE NEED TO WAKE UP AND SEND THEM A MESSAGE.** Send them a wake-up call that generations before have done. You know the names King, X, Robinson, Parks.

"We are a society made up of individuals that care about themselves. Rarely do we care about others. That has brought upon on destruction of the American Way!"

I thought, "If nothing is done about this, we will lose it all for future generations if they are even allowed to be told it."

And it went on as I started to zone out, overloading the circuits in my brain with the fact that I was becoming disillusioned again. Maybe I never stopped being so, just having hit pause.

…

And with that, the Man stepped down from the soapbox. I could hear him murmuring something over and over. It seemed like an obsessive-compulsive disorder tick. It was odd.

I could only discern a little; the Man was saying something about a book protecting him, that the book would protect him and that the book protects him. Repeated, three times three. It seemed very surreal.

With that, the Man started to fade into time, as if he had never been there.

The Man's words brought out emotions I had not felt in some time. I wrestled with them for a moment as I tried to put my finger on it. I could feel my skin temperature tick up a little (a lot).

And in an instant, the Man reminded me of how much I had questioned things in my life. The Man had reminded me of the fire I once had, now buried deep inside.

Those thoughts and emotions were snuffed out by a society of douchebags and Karens'. You know those types, themselves disillusioned by the reality around them. Just like I was.

A fire snuffed out by the Corporations, beaten down… Beaten down by the Political Establishment, the Media, and the Social Media types. The grossness that knew no bounds, a degeneration unfathomable, depravity knowing no limits.

As I sat there, I could repeatedly hear the Man's words in my mind. It agitated my core. I was furious at myself. I could see the disillusionment happening in near real-time.

111

What bothered me the most was that it was as if I had heard them before, but I could not pinpoint where. Where was the Man from?

I know I felt this way before; I'm sure of it. I know it; I could feel it in my core. My essence. Everything that made me the fucked up version of me.

I just know I had heard the Man talking to me in the past; I was so fucking sure of it. In this life, I was just so sure of it. It started to eat away at me more and more.

I took a deep breath. I looked down at my hands, clenched into fists and growing whiter and whiter. I could feel my skin tingling, a sign of losing control. Sweat was beaded on my nose.

With all I was going through in life, for all the pain and the destruction that was sadly being poured onto the populace, did I need more reason to feel this way? I mean, seriously, who needs more of this shit now?

Ahh fuck, I was angry again. Maybe I had never lost that? Had I just lost my way, forgotten it, and suppressed that part of my being? Why was I asking so many questions again? What did the Man do to me? I felt lost again.

I had tried hard to keep the darkness and anger in check for so long. The rage inside of me, that which would bring the end. The end of everything. The destroyer of worlds. The death to ALL of Man.

I was done. This was the final straw. I could no longer take, nah, handle the pressure. ***Snap*** It happened just like that. But this time, it was a bit different.

I slowly opened my hands and looked down. I could see what needed to be done. I could feel it as if I had opened the floodgates to all the voices in my head. Inside, it was uncontrollable now with no constraints.

Sweat beaded on my forehead now and slowly dripped into my eyes. My skin was ablaze, like standing outside in the desert when it was 121°. That's not pleasant, like a rectal exam from Captain Hook.

And in an instant, I let my anger take over. I saw doom, embraced the darkness and all of the pain, and now the rage was swelling inside me. I knew the time had come to embrace or defeat the darkness.

And I knew I could not defeat it. I was beaten, broken, and there was nothing left. Not even apathy could have saved me this time. And this was a complete and unconditional surrender to the darkness.

And as I stood to walk away, I couldn't shake the feeling that I knew I'd heard this Man before. So I continued to probe my feelings, knowing that … knowing that my feelings were a Harbinger.

It was time to put things in place, too; thanks, Bender, let's Kill All Humans together!

CHAPTER 13 – PURGATORY

I got home from my walk and time in the park, and a wave of electricity swept over me as I opened the door. It was so powerful that I saw a brilliant white light.

Suddenly, I'm jolted awake and find myself standing inside what appears to be a central government bureaucracy. I scan the room; its vastness does not have words.

My first thoughts ranged from "What the fuck?" to "How the fuck?" and then finally, "Seriously, what the fuck?"

First, I needed to assess where I was, the exits, the situation, and if there was any vodka. I thought of my training in such matters and then simultaneously recalled that I had never been to any training of that nature. And boom, a great quote from Lionel Hutz of The Simpsons:

I was watching *Matlock* in a bar last night. The sound wasn't on but I got the gist of it.

As I looked around, I could see people in the distance who appeared to be employees or something similar. I could only see the backsides of the people here and there, so I perceived this to be an interview process. But that view kept getting further and further away.

The place looked like some dystopian Central Government Bureaucracy, as it felt jam-packed with many workers scurrying about and people just standing, waiting. It reminded me of the DMV. Oh, bloody hell, this is a giant DMV.

As I scanned the room itself, I could not locate anything that would be an exit, best a door, window, elevator, etc. It would be easy to presume there to be no exits. Fuck, I assume that we are all trapped here. However many "we" are. I have no way to discern that, which to me, is somewhat troubling.

I stood in line, just standing here, with nowhere I could presumedly go. Perhaps I am waiting for my turn to talk to somebody, presuming this to be some sort of interview.

It's interesting; this place reminds me of what I perceived purgatory to be like, except in the form of the DMV, which itself is its own fucking hell.

Hmm, where'd I get purgatory from? Why was I thinking that? Oh shit, here comes the questions...

I stand here at what seems to be what I perceive is the back of the line, paralyzed by time as this personalized hell has no measurement. There are no clocks. There's no food or drink. It's awash with dullness, and time does not appear to move.

It's crushing. "Maybe if I had thought that far ahead, I'd known that it was a stupid decision to make," I thought. Yeah, thinking far ahead, typically a superhuman strength I had, always trapped in my mind.

But alas, I did make the decision, and I am the jackass here. Own your own shit, right?

As more time passes, or what I imagine has to be time passing, as I stand in line, waiting for an inevitable trip down somewhere other than here, I think back to Dante's Inferno. I believe Level 7: The Violent would be my destination.

Out of the corner of my eye, I saw two people entering the building. They were bland; one could not describe them to another as other than "human."

I suddenly thought, "That's odd; I didn't enter the building… Suddenly, I was just here." I had previously scanned the room and saw no door for these clowns to enter.

I further contemplate all the events that have transpired since I got "here." But let's be clear, I still don't know where here is. It feels like a DMV, a Central Bureaucracy, purgatory…

Paying no attention at first, the two humans that entered the, well, whatever/where the fuck I was, they didn't appear to be cutting line, so what the hell do I care?

Something didn't feel right to me, like bad energy or mojo. I thought, "Dude, you are in purgatory; what exactly are you expecting from the people here?" Now that was one to ponder.

Maybe it's me, but cutting in line is a bitchass move, but I couldn't place my finger on what was going on. It seemed, well, odd. Very odd, even given the current surroundings.

The two clowns appeared to have walked to the front of the line, right up to what I perceive to be the counter. I don't know if it's a help desk or receptionist, but it gave the impression as such.

I could see them, although they appeared to be a football field in length away, if not further, but that's just a guesstimate.

After an unknown period, I noticed that the two clowns that came in through the doors some time ago appeared to be doing a lot of gesticulating.

My first thought in seeing this display was to wonder if they were Italian. (I'm Italian, shut your meow hole)

My second thought was wondering if they didn't have a "number." I looked to my left, then right, and noticed a ticket counter on the wall. "Hmm, I don't have a ticket, do I?"

I look down at my hands and slowly open them up. And there is a ticket, though I do not recall getting one. Hmm.

I peer down at my ticket to see what number I have. It reads **8,675,309**. I look at the display, and it says "**420**". Are you fucking kidding me? Oh, this is punishment, all right.

After what seems like an eternity, I hear a tick. Loud, audible tick. I look in the direction of the sound and see the counter now says "421". *Fuck*! Are you kidding me? Seriously?

I sigh, take a deep breath, and wait. This is part of my punishment; it has to be. Or perhaps this was "The Powers That Be" fucking with me?

That seems likely, but I have no proof or no way of proving it right now.

After an unknown amount of time, I noticed that the two gesticulating dudes, the clowns as I believe them to be, were slowly but surely walking up towards where I was standing, although I do not think they were walking up to me.

From time to time, it appeared they were having an aggressive and passionate argument with another "person" in line. I presume it's an argument, but I had no way to hear what was going on.

I also presume I don't care as it doesn't impact me, or so I think.

The clowns continued to make their way closer and closer to where I was standing, and I could begin to hear them, although it did not make much sense. It was no language on Earth I'd have heard before.

And, of course, one of them decided to stop right next to me, slowly turning to square up and just staring at me. It was odd, but don't worry, I wasn't getting turned on.

I turned as well, standing there as I was holding my ground. There were no words, no conversation, just looking at each other. It felt like sizing up your enemy for some weird reason.

He turned to start walking away. Being the dick I am, as clown #1 took their first step away from me, I clipped one of their feet against the other. Classic.

That clown then reaches over and grabs the other one as he stumbles, eventually the two of them tumbling down towards the ground like idiots. After a few moments, the two clowns stood up. Clown #1 turned toward me, gave me a slight nod, and the two walked away. I suspect the embarrassment was enough to make them quickly walk away.

After an eternity of laughing about the clowns falling and leaving, I wonder where they went. Did they leave out of the doors they came in from? And where the fuck are those doors? How did they walk in or out? Fucking questions.

As I walk to the counter, for the lack of a better term for it, I stand in front of something, but I could not describe it other than human-like, but without any distinguishing characteristics.

I am asked, "Which direction are you going?" I pause, wondering, does this entity not know what I had just done, taking my own life to rid myself of so much pain? Does this entity just "work here"?

All sorts of thoughts flood my brain as I contemplate the ridiculousness of my fortune that I brought myself to this place with my actions and by my own will. I can't believe the stupidity of the question.

As I ponder the question that I have been asked, what would appear to be a supervisor or manager comes over and whispers something to the person interviewing me, for the lack of a better term.

It's like a scene out of a movie; I can't tell if this is a terrible comedy or a horrible tragedy. Or both. But I can know that it's awful because I am in it.

The manager turns to me and asks, "You're like a hero or something, right?"

I scrunch my face and stare at that person with a gaze that even Ghost Rider would give props to. I feel like I'm reaching out to grab its soul and take a shit on it; that's how stupid I think they are or are being.

I look at the two of them and emphatically state, "I am no hero; I am a supervillain. I destroyed the earth and billions of souls with it. Just because I trip up two jackasses, a hero, it does not make. It does not justify the misdeeds I have done. Things that I did on purpose."

God damn, oops, my sarcasm, when unleashed, it's extensive and provides me with so much joy, something I've been missing. It's been a while since I had those feelings.

And the manager said, "Well, didn't you trip them up on purpose?"

I cannot argue with someone who has seen my actions in this instance but not my overall body of work. And I finally accept, nay acknowledge, that I had done something good wherever the fuck I was.

The manager added, "You passed the test."

Seriously? What the fuck? How could anything good happen? How could any of this be real?

The manager is talking toward me now, but I have no idea what is being said. I hear bits and pieces, a word or phrase here or there. "Come back where..." and "...last known good...".

"Jebus F'ing Festivus, what is this, a Windows update?" I said with immense sarcasm. And I hear one word that brings me back to the conversation; **"store."**

Fuck, maybe I should have been paying attention. Fuck! I try to shake it off, but ever so curious still about this whatever-the-fuck-is-going-on-event. I do not understand what is going on.

I can hear them saying to me, "it is standard procedure." I just… I just don't understand. I asked once again, "How? What?" I stood there, shocked at the question I had just asked as if I suddenly got it. Like a little light bulb going off in my head.

 "Ok, fine. I have one question… How do you get in through the doors?".

And with a flash of light, this seemingly goes from bad to worser. I find myself in the body of another. They left me with my self-awareness and knowing I wasn't a 5-year-old Asian girl. Wow, they didn't prepare me for that shit.

CHAPTER 14 – AWAKENING

I slowly opened my eyes, afraid of what I would see next. And then suddenly, the only thing I noticed was…was… was… I just saw her. HER! Holy fucking shit!

She was standing there in front of me. Her arms were outstretched to me. I felt a panic attack coming on.

I could not believe that after all this time, the pain and suffering I had endured, it was her—the girl from the grocery store. I had long wondered what happened to her, secretly hoping that somehow, somewhere, I would run into her again.

And as my eyes adjusted to the environment, here I was, on that day, in that store, with her approaching me. I thought to myself, "What the fuck?" "How the fuck?" and then finally, "Seriously, what the fuck?" How?

But why here? Or now? Wait, seriously, where the fuck am I? Is this hell? Heaven… I know it's not purgatory since I was just there. Did the folks there tell me something about this happening? Oh, shit.

Was this deja vu? Was this some gift from the folks in purgatory? I don't recall them saying anything about this. Wait, shit! I feel like I'm a mess, a shit show supreme.

Was this what they meant when I heard them say "last known good"? Is this the last time and place I was happy, functioning, and better? This has to be a dream, and there's no way… And I trailed off.

My mind was starting to panic; I could feel it coming on, grasping at my soul. Here was the light walking towards me, yet I could feel the darkness coming back for me. I knew that feeling; I tried to escape it, but… I don't know where I am, when, and why I'm here. I've been through this before, wasn't I?

Still stunned, as she came in to hug me, I thought I heard her say, "Sir, I need you to… " and it trailed off, my hearing a bit sideways from the… Oh, fuck, I'm not a 5-year-old Asian girl. Right?

I wasn't sure what she said, and when she pulled herself in close, where our bodies were touching one another, not a pansy ass hug, this was the two of us… and she whispered into my ear, "Please come back to me, Punis."

ACKNOWLEDGEMENTS

Never in my life had I ever imagined that I would write a book, or two. Up until two years ago, the longest thing I'd ever written was about three pages. That was until my friend and mentor, **The Reverend CD**, challenged me to write more.

Without you, CD, nothing I have written or have yet to write, none of that would be possible if not for you. If not for that visit to the cemetery, our conversation, and how it made me think.

You are most excellent, so much so that you are the first person and sometimes the only person to read the material I've written over the last two-plus years. That covers blogs, books, and pamphlets for underprivileged reindeer.

You have been there with me when I was heading towards the gates of hell and have been the hand that pulled me back. You, and only you, have done so.

You have inspired me time and again, and you are the most influential and important person in my life in all the combined years.

You are special to me as a friend, and you damn well know I consider you a part of my family. I love you, good sir; there can be no doubt.

"**Fry**" - Besties be Besties. Thank you for all of the support you have given me. I wish I was half as good as a human, as a friend, that you have been to me.

Thank you for never discouraging me from writing this, even though it was a shit show of long, crazy… oh wait, it still is. I hope you similarly help me wherever my writing takes us, you have such a phenomenal mind.

And as my best friend for many years and through so many trials and tribulations, I love you as my brother. You know this to be true.

The Great Daniel L., You are a supremely talented artist, one whom I trust implicitly, and you know this to be true. You are also one of the few who knew about any projects I have, am, and will work on.

I also hope you know how proud of you that I am. I am honored to be your client and share parts of my life with you.

Thank you for listening to these stories over the years, even if they were scattered and told two hours at a time.

131

Oh, **Andrea**, where could I possibly start? You are such a fantastic person, someone who has known the multiplicity of this guy. The complexity of having been the OG Sapphire and someone in and around my life for so fucking long.

You said something recently while we were talking, noting that we've known one another for over one-half of our lives, 25 years now. I was blown away.

I owe you so much. Thank you for being a friend. Thank you for the OG "ass walking away moment." Thank you for knowing the most important things in life and their value over another.

Thank you for reading these works to me and for telling me what's what. I have always appreciated your candor, thoughtfulness, and drawl.

Doctor G - Thank you, you have helped me become me. No one could do what you have done for me as a human, slowly developing me into a slightly less fucked up version of myself, even if it has taken nearly 20 years.

Your patience, kindness, and love have saved me more than I can count. I thank you immensely for being there for me, human to human, so many times over many years.

Good Sister - Thank you. You have saved me twice. Nothing I do and no amount of money I could give you could ever say thank you like this. I would never have been able to create this if you hadn't saved me. I would have been stuck there, on the other side, suffering an all too similar fate.

I will only have two sisters, and we know this to be true.

Bad Sister - I surely couldn't thank Good Sister without thanking you but in a much different way. You have always been good to me from the moment I came into this world. You have never done me wrong.

Thank you for being way crazier then I am. 🙂 But seriously…

I know this isn't something I would usually say, but I wanted to say in a published book, "I love you. You are an excellent sister, and I am proud to be your brother."

I will only have two sisters, and we know this to be true.

Mrs. B - You have been to hell and back, and my hand is outstretched to you. You have dealt with massive pain and strife, and my hand is outstretched to you. You have endured, and my hands celebrate you, your strength, and the drive you have.

I am so thankful to have you in my life for so long for two reasons. First, you called me that night, worried and empathetic, knowing I had lost so much. Second, I am thankful for that birthday chat we had many years ago.

I wish I could do more to get you where you need to be, but I can only show you the love and support you have given me over the last 15+ years.

You, your most handsome husband, and Charlie are amazing. You know this to be true.

Ms. J - You are such an enigma to me, even after so many years as friends. Thank you for poking fun at this story and developing "The Department of Rules and Contracts" or DORCs with me.

I could say so many things, but more than everything, I will always cherish you, our friendship, and the drunken handholding walks.

"**Dana**" - There is no part of me that will never love you as a friend. You were there with me and experienced this story. You virtually held my hand and tried to guide this idiot. I'm sorry that I failed and went to the other side.

Without you, "**Dana**," this story would never be told. "**Dana**," without you, I'd never of lived to see "The Hello Hello Game" or the funniest of anything related to this story, #ISHBU. (See TJF2 for that shit)

I miss your Christmas cookie massacre silliness and all the fun things friends do. You are a magnificent human and will be even more astonishing as a Mom. I am so proud of you.

Thank you for being my friend, the first FLA, and rebuilding the right things in life. I'll always be thankful for all the fantastic things you brought to my life.

"**Dana**," I can say this a million times over, something that **The Great Daniel L.**, as well as **Doctor G**, both know to be true; while they got to hear the story one or two hours at a time, you lived through that with me in near real-time, and I owe you such a debt that, like **Good Sister**, I can never repay.

And lastly... <u>**Sapphire**</u> - I will be here, waiting for you on the other side.

135

BONUS MATERIAL

The other day, I was on a video call with my Secret Freezer teammates, Punis Russi, Alphonso Mango, and Misty Clouds.

We were talking about adding a little more to this book, The Other Side, and Punis, in his typical fashion, offered up something from the Tales From The Jessica Files 2 that he's working on.

I'd be an idiot if I didn't take that offer. What makes this especially remarkable is that Punis said he wrote this specifically for me. His generosity is immense, as is his compassion.

I've known Punis for a very long time, so long that it often feels like we are inside one another's heads.

Thank you kindly, my good friend. I owe you so much.

P28 - The Outcome?

Part 28, twenty-eight of The Jessica Files, a #short.
This week, we learn how crazy Punis is.

The outcome... I fear that it is something that I can see, and it is so close that I can grab ahold of it. But when I reach out, I realize it is much too far away, and I can't possibly bridge that gap.

Several years ago, I was in a very different spot before meeting Jessica. I was looking at two knee surgeries in less than two months. I knew I would put my life on hold, which was scary.

Even though I had been in and out of relationships for some time, I always knew it was because of me and not the other party, but I also knew that pain played a considerable role in my existence. Not just because I'm a Dom, but because I have shit-ass knees.

I was always hopeful that I would find somebody who fulfilled me and allowed me to take a deep breath, take a step back, open my arms and accept them into my life. I am not talking about religion, fuck those fucks.

I was fighting an inner conflict between my personality facets and the reality I lived in. I always felt like I could never win, which is why I denote that frequently. But at that time, it felt like I had something within my grasp, only to watch it slowly slip away from me, drifting further and further into an abyss.

What I was trying to grab was love, but yet no matter how far I could stretch, I could not seem to get a hold of it. It always was too far away. And that's where the subtitle comes from. Fear of not being able or even capable of bridging that gap. The one between the personalities, the voices.

In today's life, I have my Jessica, and I love her so much. I would kill all humans for her, and I will kill all humans with her. She is everything to me. She is absolute like time.

And don't give me that shit about Einstein… Time still exists; it will always exist, no matter how much you try to distort it.

In some realities, I did not get my Jessica, and I have talked about that at great lengths. In this one, though, I do have my Jessica, and I know that when I put my hand out to her as I reach for her love to pull me back, like from the other side, I know that there's a part of me that also knows that I was trapped there. I was trapped there for life.

Having spent so much time on the other side, even if it was 49 minutes and change, it was many, many years that I had to live with the constant pummeling of my soul, the constant pain. And I put my life on hold again and again and again. I didn't have my Jessica. I just had the memory of the girl from the grocery store. She was memorable, to say the least.

And now I can see a wave of pain coming for me. It will be physical or emotional, and regardless, it will be awful.

And I don't know if I can survive this. I don't know if I have enough strength left to keep going, to fight against that feeling.

This is how I felt on the other side when the darkness finally consumed me, and I could not fight it anymore. It's at one, and I just wasn't strong enough.

That is where I'm at right now in my life. The darkness is not behind me; it's all around me, and it's just waiting for me to make a mistake. It won't go away, and it was the light that Jessica brought on day one and even still today that she was able to grab hold of me and pull me back. It was her love and the absoluteness of her love that saved me.

But right now, in this world on the other side, I don't have that, and I'm facing down the barrel of a massive surgery, and I've got no one to help me. I don't have anybody to save me. I have nothing. I am on the other side and can't escape it.

It tears me apart and into smaller and smaller shreds of this guy, and I don't know what I can do to stop it. There is no light, just ever-increasing darkness. And the ever-consuming darkness that brings the nothingness of life.

Yet still, my quote remains the same. I fear that it is something that I can see, and it is so close that I can grab ahold of it. But when I reach out, I realize it is much too far away, and I can't possibly bridge that gap.

I can never get there. Not without her. And I'm afraid that all has been lost.

www.ingramcontent.com/pod-product-compliance
Lightning Source LLC
Chambersburg PA
CBHW031541310726
48971CB00008B/2573